"How long is Wren going to be with you?"

"I have no idea," Levi replied. "Her mom's in rehab for several more weeks. When she's out, she'll probably only get supervised visitation."

Oh my. "Since you're an emergency placement, won't there be a more permanent one lined up?" Savannah asked.

He shook his head. "There aren't enough permanent foster care placements in the state. I'm her guardian for the foreseeable future. That's guaranteed employment for you."

She weighed the information. Not that she had anything else lined up. The only place that hadn't called her back was the visitors' center. Levi's offer promised more money and she'd probably have more fun babysitting Wren.

"Count me in for babysitting Wren. But the reunion stuff... I don't know, Levi. Are you sure?"

He stopped chewing. Irritation flashed in his eyes.

Oh, she hadn't meant to offend him. "I didn't mean to hurt your feelings. I just want to make sure you're sincere."

"Absolutely." He wiped his hand on his napkin and reached across the table. "Do we have a deal?"

Heidi McCahan is a Pacific Northwest girl at heart but now resides in North Carolina with her husband and three boys. When she isn't writing inspirational romance novels, Heidi can usually be found reading a book, enjoying a cup of coffee and avoiding the laundry pile. She's also a huge fan of dark chocolate and her adorable goldendoodle, Finn. She enjoys connecting with readers, so please visit her website, heidimccahan.com.

Books by Heidi McCahan

Love Inspired

Home to Hearts Bay

An Alaskan Secret
The Twins' Alaskan Adventure
His Alaskan Redemption
Her Alaskan Companion
A Baby in Alaska

Opportunity, Alaska

Her Alaskan Family

Love Inspired Trade

One Southern Summer

Visit the Author Profile page at LoveInspired.com for more titles.

Her Alaskan Family

HEIDI McCAHAN

LOVE INSPIRED
INSPIRATIONAL ROMANCE

LOVE INSPIRED®
INSPIRATIONAL ROMANCE

Recycling programs
for this product may
not exist in your area.

ISBN-13: 978-1-335-93136-8

Her Alaskan Family

Love Inspired
22 Adelaide St. West, 41st Floor
Toronto, Ontario M5H 4E3, Canada
www.LoveInspired.com

Printed in Lithuania

MIX
Paper | Supporting
responsible forestry
FSC® C021394

To all those who have endured the cruelty of a mean person, you are not alone in your struggle. Remember that you are stronger than the hurtful words and actions of others.
May this story offer solace and encouragement.

Now the God of hope fill you with all joy and peace in believing, that ye may abound in hope, through the power of the Holy Ghost.
—*Romans* 15:13

Chapter One

How had she ended up here?

Savannah Morgan sighed as the familiar green forest of spruce trees flew by the truck's window. Moving home to Opportunity, Alaska, had never been on her radar, much less returning at twenty-eight, unemployed and desperate for even her old bedroom. She'd planned out her entire life with one objective—to never move back to this small town, where everyone was always wrapped up in each other's business. Until a spring break trip had morphed into a nightmare and left her without a job.

So here she sat, riding shotgun in her older brother Wyatt's pickup truck as they crossed the truss bridge that spanned the confluence of the Moose, Poplar and Kings rivers. In the distance, a swirl of white clouds obstructed the summit of Denali. The surrounding peaks of the Alaska Range were awash in the pinkish-purple light of an early-summer evening. Her hometown, nestled one hundred miles from Alaska's most glorious mountain, existed because of the many who'd gone before her, determined to find gold or silver in the nearby mines and to build a new life.

She likely wouldn't find gold or silver here, but her parents had both mentioned that the art teacher had unexpectedly retired. His position hadn't been filled. She fully intended to apply. And even though she dreaded the idea of attending her ten-year high school reunion without a plus-one, maybe going alone meant she'd be able to reconnect with Jasper Carter, the handsome guy she'd had a crush on in junior high and high school.

A fool's errand? Perhaps. But it wasn't like she had anything to go back to in Colorado. The fourth-grade teacher she'd dated for almost a year had broken up with her as soon as he'd found out she'd been fired. There was no way she'd be able to teach in the same school district. Ever. She'd subleased her apartment to a friend, sold her cheap furniture and donated her well-loved car to a charitable organization. This trip home to Opportunity was boom or bust, as the old prospectors used to say.

"I need to make a quick stop." Wyatt's voice pulled her from her thoughts. He slowed down as he approached the blinking traffic light on the other side of the bridge. "Carter's Sporting Goods has the part I need to fix my bike."

Savannah's heart blipped at the mention of Jasper's family's store. Sure, she wanted to see him, but not yet. Not like this. Including her delayed flight in Seattle, she'd been traveling for almost twelve hours. All she wanted was a shower, dinner and a place to sleep. Even if it was the bottom bunk in the cramped room she'd shared with her sisters.

"Why didn't you get the part in Anchorage?" She glanced at the coffee shop on the corner as Wyatt cruised through the intersection. They'd added outdoor seating, and strands of vintage lights decorated a new pergola. Very cool.

"Because I looked online while I was waiting for you at the airport. Carter's has it in stock, and it's three bucks cheaper."

She reached over the console and gave her brother's shoulder a pat. "Always the frugal one in the family."

"I don't know about that. My bike cost me a pretty penny, but I want to be able to hit the trails on my days off." Wyatt tapped his turn signal, slowed down and turned onto Aurora Street.

The sporting-goods store came into view, and her mouth ran dry at the sight of Carter's name on the sign mounted above the door. "Can't blame you for wanting to make the most of your free time."

"That's the spirit." The lines around Wyatt's blue eyes crinkled as he smiled. "I can be in and out in ten. You're welcome to wait in the truck."

Savannah grabbed her can of soda from the cupholder and drained the remnants. The lukewarm carbonated liquid did little to quench her thirst. She put the can back, then flipped down the visor. The mirror reflected what she'd feared. Yikes. She looked like she'd barely slept in three days. Accurate, but not necessarily the look she was going for if she was about to run into the only guy who'd made her consider staying in Opportunity. "Do the Carter twins still run the store?"

Wyatt parked in one of the empty spaces in front of the building. "As far as I know. Their sister moved to Anchorage a few months ago to work at one of the hotels, so it's just the twins and their parents now."

To be honest, she only had an interest in one particular Carter brother. Savannah quickly rebraided her strawberry blond hair. Then she fished some lip gloss and mascara from her bag and retouched what little makeup she'd applied at four fifteen that morning.

Wyatt turned off the ignition and slanted a curious look her way. "What are you doing?"

She gave her appearance another critical onceover before flipping up the visor. "Nothing."

"I've never seen you put on makeup to go into a store."

"I'm full of surprises this summer." She dropped her makeup back in her bag, slid the strap over her shoulder, then climbed out of the truck.

Wyatt didn't seem to remember that she'd had a thing for Jasper, and she wasn't about to remind him now. Or confess that back in high school, she'd doodled their entwined initials in her notebook, spent hours watching him play hockey, and cried for a solid week when he changed his mind at the last minute and went to college in Fairbanks instead of Colorado, as she'd hoped.

When she closed her eyes, she could still see the way he'd smiled when she asked him to sign the autograph section in their yearbooks that last week of their senior year. Or the thrill of their one and only dance together at the prom. Before he'd left for the after-party with her nemesis, Candace Finch.

Wyatt's sneakers crunched on the pea gravel in the parking lot as he rounded the front of his truck and joined her. "Are you sure you're all right?"

Yeah, okay, so he might've caught her daydreaming. Didn't everyone go to their high school reunion feeling sentimental about the past? What was so wrong with pulling out those comfortable memories? Reliving them made her feel good. Well, most of the time. If she didn't focus too much on what had gone wrong.

He was still staring at her. "Listen, I know you've had a rough time lately. I wanted to—"

"Please, don't." She held up her hand to interrupt. "Let's go."

She couldn't excavate those details all over

again. Or think about how rejection still hurt just as much now as it did ten years ago. Her shocking job loss had reminded her of that lesson.

Wyatt let it go. He held open the door, and she stepped inside. The familiar smell of leather sneakers, beef jerky and the rubber tires on bikes balanced on a nearby rack enveloped her. Somewhere, a phone rang, and she recognized Trent Carter, the owner, standing at the register, chatting with a customer.

"There he is," Wyatt said. "How's it going, man?"

Savannah turned, and her breath caught. Jasper Carter stepped away from an endcap and walked toward them. Wearing khaki cargo pants, brown hiking boots and a green-and-white-plaid button-down, he was the epitome of an outdoor-recreation expert. He'd cut his chocolate brown hair shorter than the style he'd embraced in high school, but those eyes... Oh, those hazel eyes were most definitely the same.

"Hi, Wyatt." Jasper's gaze flitted toward Savannah. His eyes widened. "Savannah. Hi."

"Hi, Jasper." She couldn't look away. Gone was the teenage boy of her memories. In his place stood a tall, attractive, physically fit man.

Confusion passed across his handsome features.

"Can I have more cupcakes?" A little girl, probably not even school-aged yet, raced toward them, her smudged white ballet slippers slapping against the store's linoleum floor. She wore a pink-and-purple-taffeta princess gown with a frayed hem. Chocolate ringed her mouth. She stopped beside Jasper and peered up at him, her pale blond hair twisted into two haphazard pigtails. Her hand left a chocolate smear on his pants as she patted his leg.

Wyatt and Savannah exchanged amused glances.

"Can I have another chocolate cupcake? *Please?*" She stretched out the last word and added an irresistible smile.

Jasper reached down and gently tugged on one of her pigtails. "One is enough, Wren. We're going to eat dinner soon."

"But I'm hungry now." Her mouth twisted into a frown, and her hands went to her hips. "*So* not fair."

The girl was sassy. And adorable. But seeing Jasper with his daughter planted a disappointing ache in Savannah's abdomen. If he had a child, did he also have a wife? Juicy news like that surely would've reached her in Colorado.

The door opened behind them, and Savannah instinctively stepped aside to allow the customers to enter.

"Levi Carter, are you *ever* going to answer my texts?"

Savannah froze. Even after all this time, that voice still made her want to climb right out of her skin. *Please, no. It's way too soon.*

"I need you to hand out these flyers advertising the parade." Candace Finch stopped and gave Savannah a head-to-toe inspection. Disdain pinched her flawlessly made-up features. She flipped her long platinum blond hair over her shoulder. "Savvy, is that you? Still stuck in the '90s, I see. Next time add some lipstick. Or maybe a necklace. Accessories really pull a look together."

Wyatt cleared his throat and shifted uncomfortably beside Savannah. Heat flamed her skin. She wanted to melt into the floor. She hadn't been home for twenty minutes, and she'd already encountered the one human who'd made her miserable for most of her childhood. Worse, she'd obviously made an embarrassing faux pas, mistaking Levi for his identical twin. But maybe that told her something—she was way over Jasper if she didn't even recognize this wasn't him.

And why had words failed her again? She'd anticipated running into Candace but imagined producing the perfect response. Not snarky. Not rude or thoughtless. But laced with ample confidence to let Candace know she wasn't a doormat anymore.

Was she always going to be the dorky redhead who loved art, couldn't say the right thing at the proper time and longed for the guy who longed for someone else?

How was it possible that mean girls never outgrew their need to put other people down? Levi forced his mouth into a tight-lipped smile. As much as he wanted to tell Candace she could shred her flyers and use the remnants to line her son's gerbil cage, he couldn't set a poor example for Wren. She was possibly the most observant four-year-old he'd ever met. Anything he said or did would be repeated later.

"Candace, if you can find the room, post your flyer on the bulletin board, right there with all the other local news." Levi gestured to a corkboard mounted on the wall behind Savannah. "Wyatt, I'm holding that part you need up at the counter. Speak to my father, and he'll get you all squared away."

"Thanks, Levi." Wyatt gently squeezed his sister's arm, then strode toward the counter, leaving him to help Savannah fend off any more of Candace's attacks.

"But you'll take a stack to keep beside the register, right?" Candace's bronzed forehead wrinkled. "And how about another fifty to stuff inside customers' shopping bags?"

"No," Levi said firmly. "You may post one flyer on the bulletin board. That's it."

She huffed out an exasperated breath. "I'll have to talk to Jasper about this. Stuffing the shopping bags was his idea."

Right. Levi gritted his teeth. Jasper had a habit of making quick decisions and leaving everyone else to handle the follow-through.

Levi refused to argue with Candace. She might be one of the most troublesome people he'd ever had to deal with, but he'd learned the hard way not to back down when she tested boundaries. Even though he really wanted her to leave. Especially when the woman Candace had tormented for years stood a mere few inches away.

"Welcome back, Savannah. It's great to see you."

"Thanks," Savannah said softly, her gaze skittering away.

"Lee-by." Wren pulled impatiently on his arm. "I need you."

Oh, those three little words tugged on his heartstrings. She'd only been in his life for three weeks and had somehow managed to twine him around her little finger. But he couldn't keep dragging her with him to work all summer long.

"Are you still teaching art?" Levi asked, trying to ignore Candace, who still hadn't stepped away from the conversation.

"Um-hmm." Savannah nodded, but something indecipherable flashed in her beautiful blue eyes.

"She was a teacher." Candace smacked her gum, that irritating all-knowing smirk back in place. "Heard you were looking for a new job, Savvy. Isn't that why you're here?"

Oh brother. What he wouldn't give to get Candace out of his store. Permanently.

"Savannah, may I ask your advice about something?" Levi angled his head toward the back of the store. "If you have a few minutes, we can chat in the break room."

She glanced toward Wyatt, who was still deep in conversation with Levi's dad at the counter. "Sure, let's go."

"Wren, this is my friend, Miss Morgan." Levi took Wren's sticky hand in his and led the way down the aisle with the lanterns, flashlights, headlamps and other camping accessories.

"Levi, she doesn't have to call me—"

Levi glanced over his shoulder and gave Savannah a *work with me on this* look. He didn't know much about being a foster parent. But since Wren had arrived at his house as an emergency placement, he'd learned quickly that consistency was key. Kind of like dealing with Candace.

"Is she going to stay in our house?" Wren looked up at him with those sweet pale blue eyes that had likely seen more than any four-year-old should.

"No, she has her own house."

"Your own house?" Wren twisted around to look back at Savannah. "Are you a grown-up?"

Savannah chuckled. "Sure am. Do you go to school, Wren?"

"Nope. It's summer baycation."

Levi smiled at her adorable mispronunciation. Clearly, she struggled with the *v* and *b* sounds. Was he supposed to correct her every time? Add that to his long list of questions for the social worker.

Wren tugged free from Levi and skipped into the break room like she owned the place. Which wasn't surprising, given she'd spent several hours here almost every day. Guilt pinched his insides. He had to find more reliable and consistent childcare. Soon.

Evidence of her barely supervised activities was scattered across the card table he'd set up for her. She'd abandoned a coloring page he'd printed off before they left the house that morning. There were caps off the markers and chocolate-cupcake crumbs on a paper plate. Her pink-and-purple water bottle had fallen on the floor and rolled under the cabinet by the sink.

Levi raked his hand through his hair. "Oh my. I think we need to ask Miss Morgan to help us with our not-so-secret project."

Wren squealed and jumped up and down. "I lub a project."

He couldn't help but chuckle at her enthusiasm. "Good. Because this is a big one. While I give her the details, I want you to throw that plate away and put the caps back on the markers."

Wren heaved a sigh. Her slender shoulders slumped. "Oh-kaayyy."

Savannah stood in the doorway of the break room, taking it all in. "I'm so embarrassed that I thought you were Jasper."

"No worries. Happens all the time." Levi pulled out a metal chair. "Have a seat. You should stay here for a few minutes until Candace leaves, anyway."

"Thank you for helping me escape." Savannah sat down and rested her purse on her lap. She wore black leggings, leopard-print sneakers and a graphic T-shirt featuring a popular band. He had a half dozen questions he wanted to ask about her life in Colorado, but that would have to wait.

"What's an 'escape'?" Wren dropped the plate into the trash can.

Of course she'd picked up on that. He'd have to redirect and change the subject. "Wren, put the caps back on these markers, please." Levi gestured toward the markers strewn across the table. "We need to pack up."

"Why? Where are we going?" She climbed up onto the chair beside Savannah, took the purple marker and started scribbling again.

Levi stifled another sigh. He'd been doing that a lot lately. "It's not time to color."

"But I want to finish coloring my picture."

"Fine. You may color while I talk to Miss Morgan, but then we need to go. My mom has dinner waiting for us."

"Can I get macaroni and cheese again, please?"

The girl could live on boxed macaroni and cheese. Would he ever convince her to try another option? "We'll see."

He linked his arms across his chest, leaned against the counter beside the sink and met Savannah's uncertain gaze. "I'd heard you were moving back."

Her mouth sank into a sad smile. "News has a way of traveling fast around here."

He hesitated. Was she not happy about being home?

Savannah abruptly changed the subject before he could ask. "So, what's the project?"

He drew a breath and summoned his courage. "We're supposed to design a float for the parade. The Riverside Festival is next month, and I don't have any ideas. My sister used to handle this, but she moved away, so we're up the creek without a paddle."

Dude, that was a lot. Settle. Down.

"Yeah, Wyatt mentioned that your sister had moved." Empathy filled Savannah's eyes. "That's a tough loss for your family."

"It is, but she didn't want to be here, so we're hoping she'll be happier in Anchorage. Are you interested in designing and decorating the float? I mean, I know you haven't been here long…"

She stifled a yawn. "We just drove in from Anchorage."

Argh. Lousy timing on his part. "So will you think about it?"

"I—I don't know. That's quite the task." Savannah shifted in her chair. "In case you missed

Candace's spoiler, I need a job. Something temporary until I can find another teaching position."

Oh. She meant here. At the store. "I can double-check with my dad and Jasper, but I'm pretty sure we've hired all the help we need for the summer."

Frowning, she opened and closed the clasp on her purse. "I wish I could work on your float, but I don't think I'd be able to devote the time to it right now."

"I understand."

Her gaze slid to Wren. "Seems like you've got a lot going on right now."

He palmed the back of his neck. "You're not wrong."

"Maybe we could work something out."

"Are you offering to babysit?"

"No, I'm offering to cover your shifts here while you take care of...other commitments."

"How can I convince you to change your mind?" Because spending hours trying to come up with an interesting idea for the parade float while keeping Wren occupied seemed futile.

"About the float?" Amusement flashed across her features. "You can't."

Bummer. Did she think he wanted her to handle the float all on her own? He shook his head in disbelief, though his mouth twitched with a smile. "You are tough to negotiate with."

"Yeah, well, my bank account balance doesn't allow for negotiating."

"How about waiting tables at Gunnar's? I've heard they're still hiring."

Her expression tightened, and she pushed to her feet. "Thanks for the tip."

Oh no. What had he said wrong?

"Savannah?" Wyatt appeared in the doorway, a plastic shopping bag in hand. "Are you ready?"

"Yep." Her chair scraped the linoleum as she pushed it back toward the table. "Levi was just giving me a safe space to hang out and avoid Candace."

Wait. Had he really aggravated her that much? How could she go before they'd finished their conversation? "Savannah, let's touch base soon."

"Unless I get a better offer, I'll stop by tomorrow." She offered a tight-lipped smile, then reached over and gave Wren's shoulder a gentle pat. "See you later, sweet girl."

"See you," Wren said softly.

Savannah turned and followed her brother out into the store.

"Oh boy." Levi dragged his hand over his face.

Wren eyed him. "What's wrong?"

"Nothing."

"Can she babysit me?"

"Maybe. How would you feel about that?"

"She's nice and pretty."

True. Not that her appearance had anything to do with her ability to babysit a precocious child. He needed someone kind and patient, though. Savannah had always shown both characteristics. To be honest, he couldn't remember a time when he hadn't thought Savannah was pretty, as well as kind, intelligent and incredibly creative. But he'd always suspected she'd had a thing for his twin brother, which was why he wasn't the least bit surprised when she had called him *Jasper*. He couldn't think about that now. Her interest in Jasper might've been a high school–crush thing, anyway.

Besides, he didn't even know for sure if he was allowed to leave Wren with Savannah. "Come on, Wren. Let's get going." He helped Wren put everything in her backpack. If Savannah wouldn't agree to design the parade float, he'd have to find someone else. Quickly. But he had to find *someone* trustworthy to stay with Wren too. Because he couldn't keep juggling the demands of the store and a child who desperately craved stability and attention.

"Why is finding a summer job in this town so difficult?" Savannah groaned and covered her eyes with her forearm. She'd never had trouble when she was a teenager. After dinner, she'd called four local businesses to see if they were hiring, and they'd all said no. Every single one had told her to try Gunnar's, though. Not what she wanted to hear. Been there. Done that. Still had the mortifying memories. She'd rather go completely broke than flip burgers or work the front counter at Opportunity's popular fast food restaurant.

"Levi asked you to help with the float, didn't he? Imagine spending time with such a great guy," her sister Juliet responded from the top bunk above her. "It's the perfect setup for a summer romance."

"A summer romance with the wrong brother." Regret twisted her stomach into a tighter knot. If that was possible. Worse, the alarm clock on the nightstand read 1:13 and she was exhausted. But sleep had eluded her. At least Juliet, who was home after completing her first year in college, had the energy to stay awake into the wee hours and pick Savannah's conversation with Levi apart. She'd rushed out of the store like a coward. His request for help decorating a float for Opportunity's annual parade wasn't that unreasonable. It wouldn't take much for her to come up with something clever. But she wasn't being dramatic when she'd told him she needed a job. She couldn't commit to a time-eating freebie until she knew what a paying position might require of her.

"I don't understand how Levi is the wrong brother," Juliet said. "Are you not interested because he has Wren?"

"No. I—" The hinges creaked as the bedroom door opened slowly. Savannah sat up in bed, tug-

ging the down comforter around her body. Light
from the hallway illuminated a familiar silhouette.

"Sorry if I woke you. It's just me." Their sister,
Hayley, slipped inside.

"Where have you been?" Juliet scolded her. "It's
almost one thirty in the morning."

Avoiding the question, Hayley spotted Savannah, then raced across the room. She squished
onto the mattress with a barely muffled squeal.
"You're finally home. I can't believe it."

When Hayley flung her arms around Savannah's neck and pulled her in for a hug, Savannah's throat tightened with an unexpected wave
of emotion. Oh, she'd missed their late-night chats
in this cozy room.

Hayley pulled back. Her auburn hair was
twisted into a bun and accessorized with a ball-
point pen. She wore a red T-shirt advertising the
Sluice Box, denim cut-off shorts and tennis shoes.

Savannah cleared her throat. "It's good to see
you too."

Juliet leaned over the side of her bunk, her
strawberry blond hair tumbling over her bare
shoulder. "I thought the Sluice Box closed at
eleven. By the way, you smell like french fries."

Savannah clicked on the bedside lamp. The
blackout shades their parents had installed years
ago made the room feel cave-like, keeping the
perpetual daylight of the Alaskan summer from
disrupting their sleep schedule. Not that it made a

bit of difference tonight, since they were all wide-awake.

"I stayed late to close. A guide came in with a group of climbers, and they kept us busy. Tipped well, though." Hayley unlaced her shoes and tossed them on the floor beside her bed across the room. "Anyway, we have a new manager, and his sister is in town. She's a pastry chef in San Francisco and insisted on spoiling us with a flight of rich desserts."

"Let's talk about what really matters," Juliet said, lying back down. "Did you see Max Butler?"

"He's the guide leading the climb. Why?" Hayley pulled the pen from her bun, untwisted the elastic, then raked her fingers through her wavy hair.

"You know why," Juliet said.

"But *I* don't know why." Savannah stacked her pillows against the wall and leaned against them, eager to catch up on Hayley's love life. "What's going on with Max Butler?"

"Nothing." Hayley stood and crossed the room to her dresser. "Chef made the most amazing mini cheesecakes. Oreo cookie crust, chocolate chip cheesecake, caramel topping. I'm going to have to start working out if she sticks around and keeps baking."

"Wow, sounds delicious," Juliet said. "Did you bring us any?"

Hayley took out her pajamas, then nudged the

drawer closed with her hip. "Sorry, there wasn't any left."

"You gave the leftovers to Max, didn't you? A parting gift before his next big expedition?"

"What is up with you tonight?" Hayley shook her head. "I've told you a zillion times, Max and I are friends. He's like a brother to me."

"You're a terrible liar, Hayley," Juliet teased.

"Wow, I feel like I'm missing some key details," Savannah said. "How long have you been seeing Max, Hayley?"

"I'm *not*." Hayley tossed a glare over her shoulder, then strode toward the door.

"They are meant to be," Juliet insisted. "I don't know why they're being so stubborn."

Savannah couldn't stop a smile. Wow, she'd missed the banter between her younger sisters.

"I'm going to take a shower." Hayley stopped at the door and turned back. "Oh, wait. Rumor has it you saw Levi and Wren. Isn't she adorable?"

Savannah hesitated, her arm outstretched toward the lamp. "How do you know about that?"

"I had the pleasure of serving Candace and her family tonight. She was running her mouth, as usual."

Of course she was. "I did see Levi, and I got to meet Wren. She's a handful. What's the story with her, anyway?"

"Juliet can fill you in." Hayley stepped out and quietly closed the door.

"It's sad, really," Juliet said. "Wren's mother is in a rehab facility in Anchorage, and they can't locate her father. Levi just became a foster parent recently."

"Poor Wren." Savannah blew out a long breath. "Separated from both parents. And she's so young. How terrifying."

She'd encountered dozens of situations like Wren's in just six short years of teaching. Broke her heart every single time.

"That's why you need to babysit her," Juliet said. "Give her lots of stability and attention. Then Levi will see how amazing you are and fall hopelessly in love."

Savannah turned off the light and settled under the covers. "I'm not sure I want to babysit. Or spend that much time with Levi."

"You'll change your mind. Just wait." Juliet yawned. "Sweet dreams."

Savannah stopped short of arguing. Her family knew she'd lost her job, but they didn't know all the details of what she'd endured. Frankly, she wasn't ready to share. It would be hard to keep the truth concealed forever, especially when she applied to teach again. But for now, she'd do her best to reveal as little as possible. She closed her eyes, determined to sleep. First thing tomorrow, she'd start looking for an open position. Surely someone in Opportunity needed her and was willing to pay a reasonable rate. Her parents were kind enough to let her move back in, but they expected all of them to work if they lived here. A fair arrangement, really. Besides, she certainly couldn't commit to a free project when she had to figure out who would hire her and how many hours they'd need.

Chapter Two

"Oh, Jasper. What have you done?" Levi stood in the parking lot outside Gunnar's, his personal go-to for a weekday lunch. He stared at the large block letters posted on the sign out front.

She said yes! Jasper + Miranda.

Levi pulled out his phone and checked his recent calls. To his twin's credit, Jasper had tried to call him three times in the last twelve hours. Twice after midnight and again early this morning. Levi had missed them all.

Since Wren had moved in, he had diligently silenced his phone after she went to bed so there would be no reason for sleep to get interrupted. He then neglected to check it for messages without its ring or buzz prompting him. His comfortable A-frame-style home had two bedrooms and a loft—more than adequate for himself and a child. But getting Wren settled for the night had been a challenge since day one. He'd had to eliminate all potential interruptions because more often than not, she woke up crying from nightmares. Or asking for her mom. The poor thing.

He stared at his phone, debating whether to call Jasper. His twin had mentioned a few days ago that he wanted to propose. Levi had tried to talk him out of it. And not just because his own engagement had fallen apart. But Jasper had gotten angry. Accused Levi of being selfish. He'd said since Levi was unhappy he wanted Jasper to be miserable as well. Which wasn't true. At all. So they'd dropped the conversation. He must've called to share the big news, anyway. And if Wren hadn't had a disastrous morning, followed by an epic meltdown in the store, maybe he'd be a little more excited about his brother's engagement.

Except he couldn't shake his uncertainty. Yeah, okay, so it had only been three months since Tori broke off their engagement. Maybe his heart was still a little raw. But that didn't change the fact that Miranda was barely twenty-one and had dropped out of college in the middle of her junior year because she had lofty aspirations of becoming a social media influencer. Levi turned away from the sign and crossed the parking lot toward the entrance. He rubbed his palm against the ache in his chest. He wasn't exactly jealous. More like skeptical. Jasper had lived an easy life, accustomed to getting what he wanted, when he wanted. They were business partners, but Levi and their father were forever reminding Jasper to focus on the bottom line. The store had always been about delivering exceptional products at reasonable prices to the thousands of tourists who passed through Opportunity on their way into the national park.

Sure, Jasper's outside-the-box thinking had helped them earn some extra cash a time or two. But Levi had still lost plenty of sleep over the years worrying about his twin. Not only in business but in life. And to be honest, part of him couldn't help but wonder how Savannah felt waking up to this news. Because surely she had heard by now. The whole town was probably talking about it.

He stepped inside the restaurant and took his place in line at the counter. There were at least six people waiting ahead of him. His stomach growled as the aroma of french fries and cheeseburgers wafted toward him. He should've taken his lunch break sooner, but he'd had to wait for his mom to come to the store and pick up Wren, who'd been upset when he couldn't play with her. He couldn't let her stay at the store if all she did was cry and have tantrums, though. Dad had made that very clear.

Lord, this is tough. I want to do the right thing and help a child who needs a safe place, but I don't think I'm the one for the job. Please help me know what to do next.

Praying in line while he waited to order wasn't his usual approach to a problem. Having Wren in his life had certainly driven him to pray more often. Finding reliable childcare had just zipped to the top of his to-do list. The social worker had finally returned his email and reassured him that he was allowed to hire a babysitter. Maybe there was still space available at the church's Vacation Bible School program. Wren needed attention, consistency and somebody with pocketfuls of patience.

"Hey, Levi. Give Jasper and Miranda our best. That was some proposal, right?" Mr. Wilson, who owned the white water rafting business, clapped him on the shoulder on his way to the restroom.

"Will do." Levi smiled weakly. *Some proposal?* He hadn't heard all the details. Mom would probably give him a thorough play-by-play. She'd be over the moon. At least Jasper and Miranda's engagement would take some of the focus off him. Mom and Dad had been sort of empathetic when he told them Tori had decided to attend dental school in Iowa instead of marrying him. But lately, Mom had ramped up her hints and offered more than her fair share of reminders that he should start dating again.

As if he weren't painfully aware of his unexpectedly single status.

The line inched closer to the register. Levi scrolled to one of Miranda's social media accounts. She probably had every single second of the occasion documented.

Oh my. Levi scrolled through the multiple photos and videos on her wall. Evidently, Jasper had rented one of the paddle wheel boats and staged a romantic proposal on the deck as the boat chugged down the Poplar River. How had he convinced the captain to let him string that many strands of white lights across the boat's deck? Levi blew out a long breath, then pocketed his phone. He had to admit that Jasper and Miranda looked ecstatic and very much in love in all the photos posted. Especially the one of his brother kneeling on one knee in front of Miranda, her left hand outstretched.

So why wasn't he happy for them?

After placing his order and filling his cup at the soda machine, he grabbed a straw from the stand and scanned the dining area for an empty seat. The restaurant was packed. In the back corner booth, he spotted Savannah sitting with one of her sisters. Juliet smiled when they made eye contact and waved him over. He worked his way slowly between the booths, forcing himself to stop each time someone spoke to him.

"Levi, I'm so happy for Jasper and Miranda." Sandy, who owned the general store across the street from the Carters' business, called out to him. "Such wonderful news."

"Yeah, I saw the whole proposal from the dock," Sandy's husband chimed in, exchanging smiles across the table with his wife. "That was really something."

"So I've heard." Levi forced his smile to remain in place and kept walking.

"That Miranda sure is a beauty," Sandy added. *Oh boy.* "She's a sweet girl."

He was not about to comment publicly on his future sister-in-law's appearance, because that would certainly spread like wildfire in a dry forest.

"Hi." He stopped beside Juliet and Savannah's booth.

"Here, you can have my seat." Juliet slid off the bench and stood up. "I was just leaving."

"What?" Savannah frowned. "Where are you going? You haven't eaten yet."

"I'll ask them to make mine to go." Juliet retrieved her straw handbag from the booth. "I've got to get back to work. The visitor's center is busy these days. Great to see you, Levi."

"You too," he called after her.

Juliet strode to the counter and spoke to the person bagging the orders.

Levi looked at Savannah again and shuffled awkwardly from one foot to the other. "Are you sure you don't mind if I join you?"

"It's not a problem." Savannah patted the beige Formica table with her hand. "Have a seat."

"Are you here because you're applying for a job?"

"No." Savannah's lips still held that cute lift when she smiled. "I would rather muck out stalls at the dog kennel than work here ever again."

"Wow, tell me how you really feel," he teased. "I didn't know this was such a tough place to work."

"It's probably fine." Pink tinged her cheeks. She reached for a discarded straw wrapper and threaded the paper around her fingers. "I just had a bad experience."

"Huh." He shrugged. "I don't remember."

She tipped her head to one side and tossed him a disbelieving look. "You're just being kind."

"I try to be kind, but I can't recall a scandalous story that involves you working here."

Savannah formed the wrapper into a ball. "Good, then let's not go there. Juliet offered to meet me for lunch, and I rarely say no to a chicken sandwich and fries."

"Same." He took a sip of his soda and snuck another glance at her. The navy blue and green stripes on her shirt emphasized the blue in her wide-set eyes. She'd styled her hair in loose, bouncy curls. Time had not erased the adorable freckles sprinkled across the bridge of her pert nose.

"So." She leaned her elbows on the table. "Jasper's engaged."

His heart squeezed, and he took his time swallowing his soda. "That's what I hear."

Her eyes widened. "You didn't know he planned on proposing?"

Hesitating, Levi checked the order number on

his receipt. Where was his food? He didn't want to talk about Jasper and Miranda. Not now, and not with someone he felt confident had had a crush on Jasper. "How long have you been sitting here?"

She plucked her phone from her purse. "Almost twenty minutes. Why?"

"They aren't usually this slow." He twisted in his seat and glanced toward the counter. The three employees buzzed around like bees, loading trays and filling to-go bags.

"Have they been dating long? Jasper and Miranda, I mean."

Savannah's question pulled his attention back to the conversation. "Six months."

"Oh." She lifted a slender shoulder. "Maybe when you know, you know."

Levi couldn't smother his grimace. "Jasper hasn't confided in me, and I… I don't want to speculate. Here's hoping they have a long and happy life together."

All right, so he didn't exactly mean that last part. And what was he thinking, saying that to Savannah, of all people?

Something he couldn't quite interpret flashed in her eyes.

Oh man. He was making this more awkward by the minute. Maybe he should get his order to go after all. Before she could say anything else— or got up and left—he plowed on with his offer. "Here's the thing. I still need somebody to help

me with that float. After this morning, I definitely need a babysitter for Wren. You evidently
still need a job, so how would you like to babysit
a mischievous four-year-old?"

"Seriously?"

"Wait. I have another request." His heart hammered. An idea popped in his head that might
solve two problems at once. "There's a semiformal dinner and dance at the Fairview Hotel for our
class reunion. Tori, my ex-fiancée, will probably
be there with her date, so I'd rather not go alone.
Do you want to go together?"

Her jaw drifted open. *Together?*

Levi's kind eyes held hers. Waiting. She shifted
in her seat. So many questions scrolled through
her head. "Since when is there a semiformal evening?"

"Since you-know-who weaseled her way onto
the planning committee."

She leaned closer and kept her voice low. "Candace is planning way too many things around
here."

"I couldn't agree more." He rattled the ice in
his cup. "In case you haven't checked your email
lately, she added a fifth event to the schedule."

"No, she didn't."

"A coed softball game." Levi feigned a full-
body shiver. "I think I'm busy that day."

Savannah laughed, drawing more than a few

curious glances from people sitting in nearby booths.

"Look over the events and let me know which ones you want to go to together. If any."

Her laughter evaporated. So he *was* serious. "Do you mean like a fake date?"

His chin cut upward. "I don't know that *fake* is the right word. My offer is sincere."

"I—I know you're sincere." She held up both palms. "I'm sorry. I'm just surprised, that's all."

Levi's easy grin revealed a dimple on his cheek she couldn't recall noticing before.

"You don't have to apologize," he said. "It's an unconventional arrangement."

"And what will you gain from this?"

His Adam's apple bobbed up and down as he swallowed hard. "You would totally be helping me out."

"How so?"

"My mom won't nag me about going, and I won't have to go by myself. Or deal with everyone's pitiful glances. Tori and I breaking up was a bit of a shock. To be honest, I'm still not completely over it."

Ouch. A painful breakup. Definitely relatable. "Going to any of those reunion events alone was my biggest fear. Well, that and being unemployed."

Wow, had she really just confessed that?

"If you accept my offer, you'll have both problems solved."

She looked away. He made it all sound so simple.

"Order number 137," the girl working behind the counter called out.

"That's me." Savannah plucked her receipt from the table and jumped to her feet. "I'll be right back."

Glad to have a brief reprieve from those gorgeous hazel eyes, she made her way toward the counter. She'd had trouble thinking clearly when he was sitting there, his earnest gaze riveted on her face. Or maybe his generosity had overwhelmed her. That had to be it. Because there was no way she and Levi would ever be more than friends. She respected him and admired his willingness to foster Wren on his own. But it had been Jasper's edgier, impulsive personality that had captured her attention when they were all in school together. She couldn't ignore Levi's recent breakup and obvious lingering heartache, though. Poor guy. They'd only be doing each other a favor if she said yes.

Snippets of conversation filtered through the dining area. Almost everyone was talking about Jasper and Miranda. She braced for that ugly envious feeling to seep into her abdomen, but nothing happened. *Huh.* So strange.

"One chicken sandwich, an order of fries and a chocolate chip cookie." The brunette teenage girl pushed an orange tray toward her.

"That's right." Savannah smiled. "Thank you."

"Enjoy."

Savannah added napkins and ketchup packets to her tray, then carefully walked back to their table, her mind still churning. If she told Levi no, he'd be in a tight spot. She'd have to keep looking for a job. And a plus-one for the reunion events. But was she ready to spend the rest of the summer babysitting?

Apprehension squeezed her insides. Was she obligated to tell Levi why she'd lost her job? She pushed the thought away before it grew legs.

She slid the tray onto the table and reclaimed her seat. "Want some of my fries?"

"No, go ahead." He reached for his drink again. "I'm sure my order will be up soon."

She unwrapped the paper around her sandwich, then tore open a ketchup packet and made a small pool on the corner of the paper.

"You're making me sweat bullets because you haven't answered me yet," Levi said.

"To be fair, you did give me a lot to think about and less than ten minutes to mull it over."

"You didn't see Wren's meltdown this morning. I'm a desperate man."

She lifted her sandwich and took a bite, chewing slowly. The combo of lettuce, mayo and fried chicken on a warm brioche bun tasted even better than she'd remembered. The cooks at Gunnar's refused to share the secret ingredient in their chicken sandwiches. She'd never been able to recreate the recipe or find anything that tasted nearly as good in Colorado.

"Hiring me to care for Wren is completely legit?"

"Legally, yes," Levi said. "I've already double-checked."

"All right. And what about attachment and consistency? Isn't adding a new caregiver going to set her back?"

"To be honest, she's going to have attachment issues, likely for ages. I'm no expert, but she wakes up crying and asking for her mom a lot. She never mentions her dad, and she's only been with me for three weeks."

Savannah wrinkled her nose. "That's rough. The girl has seen some things."

"I'm afraid so."

"Who has been handling your childcare?"

"Me, with some frequent help from my mom. Dad will chip in if I have absolutely no other options, but I've already tested his patience. She can't keep having tantrums in the middle of our store."

"She doesn't really belong at the store," Savannah said.

"Which is why I'd like to hire you."

Savannah reached for another fry. "I'm listening."

Levi swiped at the moisture ring left behind on the table from his drink. "I can offer you more money per hour than anything you'd make around here. Unless you're planning to work road construction."

She stopped chewing.

There was that easy grin again. "Seriously, I have a childcare stipend. It's a benefit from the state for accepting an emergency placement."

"All right," she said. "I'm intrigued."

"You want numbers? Twenty-five bucks an hour."

Whoa. She started coughing.

Levi's brows scrunched together. "Are you okay?"

She nodded, then quickly grabbed her soda and took a long sip. The drink soothed the scratchy sensation in her throat while she mentally calculated the potential payout.

He waited until she'd pulled herself together. "Like I said, competitive wages."

"It's hard to say no to that kind of money."

"Order 152!"

"Finally." Levi slid from the booth. "Be right back."

She ignored the curious glances aimed her way and focused on finishing her sandwich. They hadn't talked about how many hours a week she'd need to babysit or where she and Wren would spend most of their time.

Levi returned with his food and sat down. "The parade float… I'm sorry to tell you there's not a lot left in the budget for that. If you're willing to help, I'll take you by our warehouse and you can see what we did last year."

"I haven't come up with a design yet, but I'll need to order basics—paint, papier-mâché and streamers. I can't decorate your dad's trailer and call it good." She had to admit, she'd been tempted by his request since he made it and had even liked the idea of using her skills on a creative project that would showcase her abilities. It might help in her job hunt.

His expression brightened. "So that's a yes?"

"I didn't say *yes*. Yet. Just clarifying that I'm not capable of producing something from nothing."

He pinned her with a long look. "That's not true. I've seen your artwork. You're very talented."

"Thank you for making my point for me. Those projects all required art supplies and a substantial amount of time."

"I understand. I'm just being honest. We decided to spend more on high-end inventory to appeal to the climbers headed for Denali and cut back on some of our marketing and promotional funds. The last couple of years have been tough here. Tourism declined, so now we're more cautious than ever."

"Looks like it's going to be a great year so far. This town is hopping."

"We're hoping this trend continues, but it's only the second week of June." Levi dipped his french fry in ketchup and took a bite.

Now would be the ideal time to mention that her life had gone off the rails professionally in Colorado—not that she'd been convicted of any crimes or anything. And if she needed a background check, it would certainly be clear.

"I can see your mental wheels turning. I trust you, Savannah. I wouldn't have asked you if I didn't."

"But you also said you were a desperate man." She crumpled up her sandwich wrapper. "Which implies you're running out of options. Since we're being honest, I'm really not sure I'm ready to spend forty hours a week with a four-year-old."

But the money he offered was good. Really good. And she did *not* want to work in a restaurant. No matter how many chicken sandwiches she'd get to eat for free, it wouldn't be enough.

Levi finished chewing a bite of his cheeseburger. "I don't expect you to spend forty hours a week babysitting. How about we do twenty with Wren, and then you can let me know when you're available for the float?"

"I do need to let you know that I want to apply for the art teacher position since Mr. Golden retired."

"Good for you," Levi said. "You definitely should."

"Do you know how long Wren is going to be with you?"

"I have no idea. It will be through the end of

July, for sure. Because even if they locate her dad, it will be weeks until there's a hearing and the judge allows him to have his parental rights restored. As far as I know, her mom's in rehab for several more weeks. When she's out, she'll probably only get supervised visitation."

Oh my. "Since you're an emergency placement, won't there be a more permanent one lined up?"

He shook his head. "There aren't enough permanent foster care placements in the state. I'm her guardian for the foreseeable future. That's guaranteed employment for you."

She weighed the information. Not that she had anything else lined up. The only place that hadn't called her back or given her a straight answer was the visitor's center. Levi's offer promised more money, and she'd probably have more fun babysitting Wren.

"Count me in for babysitting Wren and designing the float. But the reunion stuff... I don't know, Levi. Are you sure?"

He stopped chewing. Irritation flashed in his eyes.

Oh, she hadn't meant to offend him. "I didn't mean to hurt your feelings. It's very sweet of you to offer, and I don't want to go by myself. I just want to make sure you're sincere."

"Absolutely." He wiped his hand on his napkin and reached across the table. "Do we have a deal?"

She shook his hand, noting the pleasant sensation of his strong, calloused fingers in hers. *Oh brother.*

"Well, well, well. What do we have here?" Candace stopped beside their table, her knowing smile infuriatingly wide as her gaze landed on their hands still laced together. "It seems like there's more than one Carter twin with fun news to share."

Savannah opened her mouth to object, but Levi's foot found hers under the table and gave a very clear *go with it* nudge.

"Your timing is impeccable, as always, Candace." Levi's patronizing tone was lost on the nosy woman. "Can we help you with something?"

Candace's smile dimmed. "Just wanted to remind you that the deadline to purchase tickets for our big formal reunion event is coming up. Wouldn't want you two to miss out."

Savannah choked back a laugh. How did the woman manage to sound so sincere when she couldn't possibly mean what she said?

"Noted." Levi's thumb caressed the back of her hand, sending a delightful sensation zinging up her arm. "We'll be there."

Candace's mouth opened, then closed. "Great. Talk soon, then."

As soon as Candace walked away, Savannah slid her hand away from his. "What. Was. That?"

Eyes bright with amusement, Levi lifted one shoulder in a casual shrug. "That was me putting our plans in place."

"Levi, I don't think—"

"Don't worry. We're not hurting anyone. Besides, her world revolves around talking about people. She'll move on to something else by dinnertime." Levi picked up the last remaining bite of his burger. "All kidding aside, thank you for helping me. You have no idea how much this means to me. And to Wren as well."

What had she gotten herself into? From the corner of her eye, she spotted Candace chatting with three of their former classmates. Four pairs of eyes swiveled their way. An icy ball of dread lodged in her belly. Levi had been right. Candace hadn't wasted time spreading the word.

Savannah managed to find her voice. "I promise I'll take good care of Wren."

Doubt twisted her insides, reminding her of the last time she'd made a similar pledge and failed miserably. Or committed to keeping a deeply personal secret. She tamped down the negative thoughts and forced confidence she didn't feel into the smile she offered her new fake boyfriend. She could do this. For Levi and for Wren. No one ever needed to know about her past missteps.

Chapter Three

The next morning, Levi rushed to get ready for work. He'd overslept and now had less than ten minutes before Savannah would be here to stay with Wren for the first time.

And it was way too quiet.

He hung his wet towel on the rack, ran his fingers through his damp hair and then opened the bathroom door. Yep. Too quiet.

"Wren?"

No answer.

"Wren, are you still watching your show?"

Nothing.

He'd agreed to let her watch one episode of her favorite animated show after she'd finished eating her breakfast. Had she muted the volume? He hurried out of the master bath and into the living space. He blinked against the sunshine streaming through the wall of windows to his left. The television had been turned off. Wren's well-loved pink-and-white-striped blanket sat abandoned on his gray microfiber sofa.

"Wren?"

"I'm right here."

Her exaggerated whisper made him smile. "What are you doing?"

She didn't respond.

His chest tightened, and he followed the sound of her voice into his small kitchen. What in the world? A trail of sugar led from the cabinet beside the stove across the laminate floor to an alcove where he'd had a desk built into the custom cabinets. Wren had quickly claimed the spot as her own on her first day living with him, so he'd complied and stowed his chair away in the shed out back. He didn't have time to sit at the desk anyway.

The frayed edge of Wren's princess dress and her bare feet revealed her location. He sank down beside her, carefully avoiding the sugar trail.

She had slid back against the wall. A plastic mixing bowl, a whisk and what was left of a five-pound bag of sugar sat beside her.

"What are you making?"

"I wanted to make cookies." She hung her head, refusing to look at him. "With sugar. I couldn't remember the rest. And I'm not supposed to use the stobe."

He drew a deep breath and silently prayed for the right words. Her mispronunciation of the word *stove* tickled him. It was hard to be annoyed when she looked so cute. Should he praise her for not using the stove or firmly remind her that she wasn't supposed to bake without a grown-up?

"All right, pumpkin. Scoot on out of there, please. We need to clean this up. Quickly."

Her chin shot up. "But what about my cookies?"

He extracted the whisk and the bowl. "Come on. Let's start by washing your hands. Miss Morgan will be here soon."

"Will she help me make cookies?"

"Maybe." Pushing to his feet, he set the bowl on the counter. "I'm not sure we have the ingredients."

"Because I used all the sugar," she wailed, her eyes filling with tears.

Oh no. Please, not the crying. Not now. "We can get more sugar if we need to."

"Today?" she sobbed, sliding out from her hiding spot.

"I—I don't know. Right now, I have to get ready to go to work. Miss Morgan will be here any minute."

He pulled the step stool he'd bought for Wren closer to the kitchen sink. "Hop up here, kiddo. Let's wash your hands."

She obeyed, but her little body trembled as she gulped in a raspy breath.

Why was she so upset about the sugar and the cookies? He made a mental note to reach out to his case worker about the frequent meltdowns. First, he'd ask Savannah. She probably had some insight to share from her teaching experience.

He turned on the water and tested the temperature before Wren put her hands under the spigot.

"Can we sing the birthday song?"

Smiling, he squirted hand soap into her open palms. "Sure. Rub, rub, rub."

She slicked the suds back and forth, her blue eyes riveted on his.

"What's the matter?"

"You start," she said.

"First, I need to make sure it's not your birthday. I'd feel terrible if I missed it."

She shook her head. "My birthday is October twelve."

"Phew." He pressed the back of his hand to his forehead. "I was worried there for a second."

She tipped her head back and giggled. "No, silly. But we're supposed to sing the song when we wash our hands."

"Oh, right." He added soap to his own hands. "Tell me again why we sing?"

"Because that means we gots all the germs," Wren said.

"Perfect. Okay." He cleared his throat, then joined her in singing a terribly off-key rendition of the birthday song. When they were finished, he pulled the blue-and-white-checkered towel from the cabinet and helped her dry off.

"Do you know where the broom and dustpan are?"

She shook her head.

"Let me show you." He helped her off the step stool. Through the kitchen window, sunlight reflected off a car as it pulled into his driveway. "Miss Morgan is here."

"Can we go to the park?" Wren skipped beside him as he led the way toward the closet in the hallway where he kept his housecleaning supplies.

"I have to go and work at the store. Miss Morgan's going to take care of you, remember?"

"Let's ask her if she'll take me to the park." Wren hopped from one foot to the other. "Can we take snacks and a juice box?"

"We'll see." He opened the closet. "This is the broom and the dustpan."

"They're so little," she said, scrunching her nose.

"They'll get the job done." Levi handed her the plastic dustpan with the small brush attached. "Let's go clean up that sugar together."

"But she's at the door," Wren said. "I heard the knock."

"Let's invite her in, and then we need to clean up." He set the dustpan and broom down; then they crossed to the door together. He pulled it open. His breath hitched. Savannah looked especially cute in a pale pink T-shirt, dark-washed jeans and white sneakers. Her hair glinted in the sunlight, and the ends of her ponytail bobbed against her shoulder. She smiled. "Good morning."

"Good morning, Miss... Wait." Wren looked up at him, a tiny wrinkle in the space between her pale eyebrows. "What do I call her again?"

Her loud whisper drew laughter from Savannah. A sound even sweeter than he remembered.

Before he responded, Savannah spoke up. "I'm her babysitter, not her teacher. Why can't she call me Savvy?"

"Sabby." Wren giggled again, struggling with the *v*'s. "That's funny."

Levi stepped back and motioned for Savannah to come inside. "If that's what you think is best, she may call you by your first name."

"It *is* what I think is best." Savannah offered him a *don't worry, I've got this* look, then put her hand out. "Wren, give me five. We're going to have so much fun."

Wren slapped Savannah's outstretched palm with a loud smack.

Savannah feigned a grimace. "You're strong."

A quick glance at the clock sent panic surging through him. Wow, he was late. Not that it was a huge deal. It was Dad's turn to open the store this week. Still, he couldn't forget the barbed comments Dad had made since Wren moved in. He'd stopped short of saying he wasn't pleased with Levi's decision to become a foster parent. But the message was still loud and clear. He'd simply have to prove his father wrong. This wasn't a choice he'd made lightly. Given the option, he'd provide refuge for any child who needed a safe place.

"Sabby, can we go to the park?" Wren tugged her blanket from the back of the sofa and clutched it to her chest. "With juice boxes?"

"Let me show her around first," Levi said. "Then you can plan your day together."

Wren didn't answer. Instead, she wrapped her blanket around her shoulders and hummed softly. Already distracted. He debated reminding her to sweep up the sugar. Not a task she'd handle independently. He'd have to take care of it later.

"Why don't you pick out a couple of books to look at while you wait?" Savannah suggested. "Then we'll chat about the park."

"And the juice boxes?"

Savannah smiled. "And the juice boxes."

Wren skirted the end of the sofa, dropped her blanket on the carpet and then pulled out a basket of books from the shelf under the television. One by one, she took every book from the basket and spread them on the floor.

"Oh my." Levi dragged his hand over his face. "The messes. They just don't stop."

"That's all right." Savannah offered an empathetic smile and gently squeezed his arm. "I'll help her clean up."

He couldn't help but notice that he enjoyed the

warmth of her hand on his bare arm. Not that he'd admit that now. Instead, he angled his head toward the sugar trail. "By the way, guard the sugar closely."

She craned her neck and surveyed the kitchen. "Noted. What happened?"

"She decided to make some cookies while I was taking a shower. Thankfully, she reminded me that she knows not to use the stove."

Savannah tucked her hands in her back pockets. "She gets credit for safety awareness. I'll limit personal grooming time to less than thirty seconds, though. Just to be extra safe."

Levi chuckled. "You're allowed to take bathroom breaks."

"Okay, what else? Any allergies? Does she take any medication?"

"No and no. She just has a lot of energy." He retrieved the broom and dustpan, swept up the sugar, and disposed of it in the trash can under the window. "I wrote down my phone number, my mom's number and the number at the store."

"How about Poison Control and Search and Rescue?" Savannah teased.

Warmth crawled up his neck. Yeah, okay, so maybe he'd gone a little overboard. "I'm just making sure you have everything you need."

"I'm sorry," Savannah said. "I shouldn't make jokes. Thank you for the information. I promise

I will take excellent care of Wren, and we'll have a great time."

Levi lifted his keys from the basket on the counter and pocketed his phone. "There are plenty of options for lunch in the fridge and the pantry. She'll try to get you to make her macaroni and cheese, but you don't have to. In case you haven't noticed, she wants to go to the park. Her nap time is at one thirty, and—"

Savannah held up her hand to interrupt. "Levi, I've got this. You can go."

"Right. Thanks again." Flustered, he scooted past her on his way to the door. "See you, Wren. Be good."

She didn't even look up from her book. "Bye."

He left and jogged to his truck, keys jangling in his hand. For the first time in three weeks, a sense of calm washed over him. Thanks to Savannah, he had the freedom to focus on his job at the store instead of constantly dividing his attention and feeling guilty. He was still surprised she'd agreed to help him at all. Admittedly, his method for convincing her had required confessing he still wasn't over Tori, something he wasn't thrilled about sharing. But Savannah seemed like she could use a friend. Besides, maybe taking good care of Wren, managing his responsibilities at the store and showing up for reunion events would prove to himself and everyone else that he'd bounced back from his failed engagement.

* * *

Wow, the girl really loves that dress. Savannah carefully set the filthy princess dress on top of Levi's washing machine in the hallway closet. It had taken quite a bit of persuading, but finally, she had Wren convinced that a pair of pink leggings and a pale blue T-shirt would work better for a trip to the park.

"Wren?" Savannah crossed to the spare bedroom and knocked softly on the closed door. "Have you finished changing?"

The muffled sound of paper crinkling made her pause and lean closer. "It's time to leave. Are you ready?"

Wren opened the door. She refused to meet Savannah's gaze. A guilty expression drifted across her face. She was wearing the clean clothes, like they'd discussed, and she'd accessorized with a ball cap advertising a team Savannah had never heard of. No worries. Fashion and rooting for a particular team were not her concern. Getting that dress washed had been her angle.

Before turning away, she quickly scanned the bedroom. Wren blocked the doorway and had her hands behind her back. Was she hiding something?

"Do you need to use the bathroom before we go?"

Wren nodded, then scooted past her and darted into the bathroom. Once the door was closed, Savannah stepped into the bedroom. *What a cute space for a little girl.* A twin bed with an adorable pink-and-white comforter shoved to the end sat against the opposite wall. Levi had added a matching white dresser, nightstand and desk. Someone had hung white curtains dotted with small pink flowers over the window. A small red cardboard box wedged between the nightstand and the bed caught her eye. She moved closer. It was a variety pack of snacks. The box top had been ripped off. Only three packages remained. Savannah lifted the pillow on the twin bed and found another pack of cookies stashed there.

Her chest pinched. *Oh, Wren. Why?*

The toilet flushed. Savannah hurried out into the hall. By the time Wren had emerged from the bathroom, Savannah was already back in the living room. She'd focus on keeping Wren safe today. Now was not the time to confront her about the hidden food.

"I heard there's a fantastic pirate ship at the park. Have you seen it yet?" Savannah picked up the insect-repellent container Levi had left for her on the counter and tucked it in the side of Wren's backpack.

"Nope." Wren bopped around Levi's living room, twirling and humming. Savannah stopped and surveyed the rustic A-frame. Modern furniture, neat stacks of books and a few framed photos made it feel like a home. The vaulted ceilings and broad expanse of windows granted a breathtaking view of the mountains. A grassy meadow offered privacy from Levi's closest neighbors. Through a line of mature trees, she glimpsed a section of the Poplar River flowing lazily through his property.

"Can we go now?" Wren stopped twirling and hurried toward her. "I'm bored."

"Yep. Let's do it." Savannah skimmed the notes Levi had left one more time. Lunch packed. Sunscreen, water bottle and emergency contact info all present and accounted for. She swung Wren's pink-and-purple backpack onto her shoulder. "We're ready, kiddo."

"Can we have milkshakes after?"

Savannah hesitated. Levi hadn't mentioned anything about that. "Milkshakes. Where?"

"At the milkshake place."

Savannah stifled a smile. "We'll see. But lunch first. And Levi says that you also have an afternoon nap. Is that true?"

Wren pushed out her lower lip.

Savannah waited. *Please tell the truth.* She so wanted Wren to trust her enough to be honest.

Finally, Wren nodded. "I get in my bed for one hour. But I don't always sleep."

Savannah patted her shoulder. "Thank you for telling me the truth, Wren. Good job. Can you put on your shoes?"

"Uh-huh." She hurried toward the door and

shoved her feet into a pair of canvas sneakers she'd plucked from a small rack. "Okay, I'm ready."

"Same." Savannah double-checked that she had the key Levi had left for her, then held the door open for Wren. She hurried outside, stopping short when a gray minivan pulled in the driveway.

"Someone's here," Wren said, immediately darting back behind Savannah and clutching the tail of her shirt.

Savannah's scalp prickled. "Do you know that car, Wren?"

"No," the little girl whispered.

Savannah's pulse sped up. No need to panic. It wasn't unusual for a child who'd experienced trauma to be wary of strangers. That didn't mean she had to be. The door opened, and a woman stepped out. Savannah recognized her familiar hairstyle and blew out a relieved breath. "That's Levi's mom."

"Oh." Wren inched out from behind Savannah and twined her arms around the porch railing. "I don't remember that car."

"Hello there." Leanne Carter moved toward them, carrying three disposable containers with lids in her arms. "Savannah, I'm so happy to see you again. Welcome home."

"Thank you. Mrs. Carter, have you met Wren?"

"I sure have. Hey, sweetie."

"Hi." Wren pointed to the containers. "What's in there?"

Leanne picked her way across the driveway, a pleasant smile on her round face. "I brought some meals."

"We're going to the park," Wren said, her little hand finding its way into Savannah's.

"Oh. Well, I'm glad I caught you." Leanne stopped in front of them. "These need to be refrigerated."

"I haven't locked up yet." Savannah gestured toward the door with her thumb. This was odd, pretending she had control of Levi's house, when his mother probably came and went all the time. Using her own key.

"Perfect. Come in with me, and we can chat."

Savannah hesitated. "Wren and I need to go. It's a bit of a walk down to the park."

"I can drive you. This will just take a minute," Leanne called over her shoulder as she managed to get the door open without dropping anything. "Besides, we need to catch up."

"Why do we have to go back in?" Wren whined. "This is taking forever."

Savannah dipped her head toward Wren's. "Patience, please. We'll get going soon. Levi's mom is doing something nice, and we need to be grateful."

Wren shot her an annoyed look but followed Savannah back inside.

"I just wanted to say again how happy I am that you're home," Leanne said. "Your family must be thrilled—especially your mom, to have all her birds back in the nest."

Wren slammed the door.

Savannah turned and pulled the little girl close to her and gave a gentle squeeze. She couldn't blame her for her outburst. "Keep your shoes on, sweet pea. We're going to go in just a minute."

If Leanne noticed that Savannah hadn't answered, she didn't react. She'd already headed into the kitchen, obviously quite comfortable in her son's home. Savannah shifted awkwardly from one foot to the other.

"I want to go now," Wren insisted. "I'm getting hungry."

"I know." Savannah patted her shoulder. "Me too."

"We're having a party tomorrow night to celebrate Jasper and Miranda's engagement. I'd love for you to join us." Leanne opened the fridge and put the containers inside.

Savannah's stomach twisted. "I'll have to check my calendar."

She happened to be 100 percent certain there wasn't a thing on her calendar tomorrow night, but she couldn't quite come up with a plausible excuse. Levi hadn't mentioned it. Did he want her there? Was he planning on going? Surely his mother wouldn't stand for him to skip it. If Leanne Carter was having a party, especially an event honoring one of her children, she always expected half the town to attend. Still, Savannah would be quite happy to not celebrate Jasper's proposal to Miranda.

"I'll speak with Levi." The words were out before she'd given careful thought to how they'd land.

Leanne shut the door and clapped her hands together. Her whole face beamed with excitement. "I'm just so tickled that the two of you have been able to reconnect."

"I'm not—I mean, we're not—"

"We haven't wanted our Levi to be alone." Leanne kept talking, as if Savannah hadn't said a word. "I don't have to tell you what a catch he is, but he sure has taken his sweet time settling down. Of course, Tori threw us all a curveball when she called things off."

Savannah's face heated. Oh, she did not want to have this conversation. Not now. And not without Levi to help her deflect his mother's comments. "Mrs. Carter, I'd love to stick around and visit, but I really need to get Wren to the park so we have enough time to play before she has to come home for her nap."

"Oh, of course." Leanne's smile dimmed. Her gaze drifted to Wren. "Sorry to interrupt."

Savannah winced at her tone. "You're not interrupting. It's important to me to keep Wren on her routine."

"What's a routine?" Wren pulled on the hem

of Savannah's shirt, her eyes toggling between the two of them.

"All right. I'll be on my way." Leanne rattled her keys and moved past them toward the door. "Did you want a ride?"

"No, thanks." Savannah pasted on a smile. "It's a beautiful day for a walk."

"Don't forget. Our house, tomorrow at six thirty. Dinner will be served."

"I'll keep that in mind. Thanks for the invitation," Savannah said.

"Bye-bye." Leanne waggled her fingers before slipping outside and closing the door.

Savannah reached for her phone to text Levi but changed her mind. Wren deserved her full attention. Besides, after their conversation at Gunnar's about Jasper and Miranda, she wasn't sure if he was going to the engagement party. Wren's early bedtime gave him the perfect reason to decline. Except Levi and Jasper had always been quite close—at least, that's how she'd remembered them. Even if Jasper's proposal had caught Levi by surprise, she couldn't fathom him skipping the celebration. If she went, would it be their first outing as a "couple"?

Levi flicked his blinker on, slowed down and then turned onto the road leading to his parents' property.

"Whoa." He promptly tapped the brakes. Cars

lined both sides of the street, packed in bumper to bumper.

"Are these all your friends?" Wren's question drew a soft laugh from Savannah, riding in the passenger seat.

"My brother Jasper's friends," Levi said, shifting into Reverse and eyeing an open spot uncomfortably close to the mailbox.

"It's not too late," Savannah said quietly. "You can still execute a three-point turn, whip this thing around and leave. The next episode of *Yellowstone* is calling our names. I'll even make the popcorn."

Was she serious? Those were the most words she had spoken since he'd picked her up at her house fifteen minutes ago. "Thank you for coming with me. You obviously had other plans tonight."

The corners of her mouth twitched. "What can I say? Your argument was very persuasive."

"We didn't argue." He guided his car into the spot, narrowly missing the bumper of the truck in front of him. "I acknowledged your generous offer to stay with Wren, but there's no way I'm doing this by myself."

"So this is part of our fake-dating scheme?"

His chest tightened at her casual use of the phrase. He pressed a finger to his lips and discreetly tipped his head toward Wren in the back seat. After shifting into Park, he snuck a quick glance over his shoulder. Wren was flipping through the pages of a coloring book. She didn't look up or ask any questions.

"We need a safe word." He turned off the ignition. "Wren, don't forget your jacket."

Savannah got out first and circled around, joining him on the driver's side. "A safe word?"

"You know—a word or phrase we say to each other when one or both of us want to leave."

"How about, *I don't want to be here*?"

Levi rolled his eyes before opening the back door and helping Wren out of her car seat. She thrust her purple hoodie toward him.

"Nope, that's for you to carry." He shut the door. The three of them walked down the road together. Denali and the mountains flanking it rose up out of the tundra like a wise council of elders, presiding over the land. Snow-capped peaks pressed toward a pale blue evening sky. The sun left pink and coral-colored streaks in its wake as it inched its way toward the horizon, sinking lower but never setting this time of year.

"You look nice tonight," he said. For someone who didn't want to attend, Savannah had made an effort with her appearance. She'd chosen a blue short-sleeve shirt with puffy sleeves, jeans and soft brown slip-on loafers. Her hair was pinned up in a clever twist, and he had to stop himself from staring at her slender neck and delicate collarbone.

"Thank you," Savannah said. "You look nice too."

"Can we all hold hands?" Wren walked between them, the skirt of her taffeta princess dress flitting around her bare legs.

"Thank you for washing her dress." Levi took Wren's hand in his.

Wren grabbed Savannah's hand. "Yes, thank you. Now, swing me, please."

They complied with Wren's request and lifted her gently into the air between them.

"It's going to be all right," he said. "We don't have to stay for long."

Savannah eyed him. "Promise?"

"Promise. Wren needs to be in bed by nine."

"Yay!" Wren squealed with delight. "I get to stay up for more minutes."

Savannah pressed her lips together.

He tightened his grasp on Wren's sweaty palm. "It's a special occasion, right?"

Savannah didn't answer. His forced enthusiasm made the knot in his stomach cinch tighter. Why did he feel the need to make this all sound better than it was? Maybe he'd been selfish, getting her to come with him tonight.

"Come on. This will be fun."

"Hope so," Savannah said, gently lifting Wren into the air one last time.

To be honest, he still wasn't completely on board with Jasper and Miranda's decision to get married. But Jasper had let him know when they spoke at the store that he was overjoyed. So Levi would fake it until his emotions got in line.

The sound of laughter and music mingled together in the air as they reached the front porch of his childhood home. A sign staked in the lawn indicated they were supposed to go around back. Except for his sister, who'd insisted she couldn't come home on short notice, he anticipated seeing almost everyone who knew and loved Jasper gathered in their backyard. Including Tori.

He led the way around the side of the house and stopped short. His ex-fiancée stood in the middle of the yard, her hand tucked into the crook of another man's elbow. Savannah bumped into him, her hand finding purchase at his waist. He silently willed Tori to notice, but she didn't even make eye contact.

"Oops, sorry," Savannah said and stepped away. Cool air filled in the empty space she'd left behind. Conversation stuttered as people spotted them, then went back to chatting when they realized he wasn't Jasper. Levi shifted from one foot to the other, instinctively reaching for Wren. There had to be at least a hundred people here. He should've prepared her for a crowd this size.

"Do you know all these people?" Wren asked, drawing a chuckle from a couple standing nearby.

"Most of them," Levi said, keeping his tone light. "Let's find something to drink."

They made their way to the coolers on the

ground near the patio. He lifted the lid and offered Wren a juice box.

"I'll take water, please," Savannah said.

Levi grabbed water for her and a soda for himself. Drinks in hand, they moved off to the side to make room for others to access the coolers.

"Can I play?" Wren pointed to the old play structure his parents had never disassembled.

"Sure." Levi took the unopened juice box she pushed into his hand. "Have a good time." Alone with Savannah, he drew a deep breath and forced himself not to look at Tori. Or the guy she'd brought to the party. Thankfully, plenty of folks milled about. Maybe they wouldn't even cross paths.

He set the juice box down on the patio and intentionally angled his body toward Savannah. "Things are going well with Wren so far?"

She nodded. "It's only been two days, but we're having fun together."

"Good." He popped the top on his soda. "She talked about you nonstop at dinner last night. Until she fell asleep at the table."

Savannah smiled. "We played outside for a long time. I was convinced I'd worn her out, but then she refused to take a nap."

"She's fiercely devoted to not napping."

Savannah's expression grew serious, and she leaned closer. "There's something I wanted to talk to you about."

Uh-oh. "What happened?"

"She hoards food, Levi. There's a box of snacks stashed in her room, and there are empty wrappers in the bottom of her backpack, and I found more cookies hidden under her pillow."

His eyes roamed her face. "I hadn't noticed. What should I do?"

"I'm not sure." Savannah shrugged. "She's so sweet. It breaks my heart."

"Aw, look at you two lovebirds." Jasper's unexpected arrival and his careless words landed like a bucket of ice water, dousing their conversation.

Savannah's eyes widened.

Levi winced and guarded his drink as Jasper slung his arm around his shoulders. "Everyone's been asking about you, bro."

"I think you're mistaken. Tonight's about you."

"No, no, no." Jasper laughed, shaking his head. "Me and my girl are old news. You're the ones everyone's talking about. I have to say, I'm pleasantly surprised."

Savannah gave a small gasp. Levi silently willed his twin to back off. *C'mon, man. Don't do this.*

"What's surprising?"

"You. Making spontaneous decisions like it's your job. Since when are you two a couple?" Jasper's gaze bore into him. Levi tipped his chin up, refusing to give Jasper any of the details he was digging for. They'd barely talked at all in the last few days. Besides, he didn't owe his brother an explanation. About anything. Jasper certainly hadn't consulted him before he'd gone and put a diamond on Miranda's finger.

"Relax, all right? You don't need to make a big deal about us," Levi said, trying to keep his voice low.

"Oh, but I do," Jasper insisted. "Especially since Tori's here with her new man as well. So why not give the people what they want?"

Levi's mouth ran dry. The less he said, the better.

"Don't look at me like that." Jasper clapped him on the back. "We want to know that you're really together. So convince us. Go on—kiss your girl."

Levi's stomach plummeted to his toes. This couldn't be happening.

Chapter Four

Her legs trembled with the need to run. But she'd
tried that before—leaving Colorado behind and
seeking refuge in her hometown. Two days in, and
she'd already encountered a speed bump or three.
She stood frozen in place, squeezing her bottle of
water so hard that it crackled. What was Jasper
doing? Why had he just dared Levi to kiss her?
They weren't really a couple. Surely Jasper knew
this. Didn't he and Levi have some unique twin-
to-twin communication? Maybe Levi hadn't had
time to explain to his family that she was helping
out with Wren, as well as designing and building
the float that none of them seemed to have time
to tackle.

Levi slid his arm around her shoulders, sending her pulse into overdrive.

He wasn't going to kiss her for the first time
in front of everybody because Jasper had dared
him to. Was he?

They had not discussed this. Yes, he'd asked
her to attend certain events with him since his ex

hadn't moved away yet, and they'd mentioned fake dating in the car on the way here, but they hadn't explored the details of the far-fetched plan. And while the sixteen-year-old version of her would flip out at the thought of a spontaneous kiss with one of the Carter twins, this was reality. A very public reality, with most of Opportunity claiming their proverbial front-row seats to her drama. Honestly, her daydreams had never been about Levi— although, at this moment, he smelled like clean soap and trees, and she kind of liked the warmth of his fingertips as they gently caressed her arm.

"Savannah and I are just getting to know each other again," Levi said, the tenderness in his eyes evident as his gaze found hers. "We're taking things slow."

Oh, she could definitely hug him for navigating his brother's obnoxious behavior without faltering. Especially since Jasper's deep voice had carried, and her skin was heating up under the weight of people's curious stares.

She cleared her throat and then managed a wobbly smile. "Right."

"Lee-by, I need you."

Wren's desperate cry reached them, and Levi's eyes widened. "I have to help her. Will you be all right?"

Swallowing hard, she nodded.

"Be back in a second. Don't let him get to you," he whispered. Despite the anxious knot pulled tight in her abdomen, the warmth of his minty breath on her cheek and his kindness sent a pleasant sensation zipping through her.

Sadly, Jasper hadn't moved at all.

"You okay there, Savvy?" His eyes dipped to her hands. "Need more water or something to eat?"

She tipped her chin up, determined to follow Levi's example and deflect Jasper's comments. "No, thanks. I'm fine for now. Congrats on your engagement. That's exciting. You must be so happy."

Jasper's tight smile gave her pause.

"Yeah, we're over the moon." He stepped closer, and his smile vanished. "Do you want to tell me what you're up to here?"

An icy chill danced along her spine, and for the second time since she'd arrived, she desperately wanted to leave. But he had her cornered against the patio furniture, and she wasn't about to make a scene. "Sorry?"

"What brings you back to town? Surely it's not a summer romance with my twin brother."

Wow, when had he gotten so blunt? She twisted the cap off the water bottle and took a long sip. Jasper didn't get the hint. He kept standing there, his piercing eyes boring into her.

"We're having a class reunion, remember? And since you and Levi clearly haven't had a chance to chat, I'm going to babysit Wren and, in my spare time, design and build a float for your store. Evidently, the deadline to post your entry for the festival is closing in fast. The parade's less than three weeks away."

Too snarky? Probably. But his questions and his attitude unnerved her.

Jasper rubbed his fingertips along his angular jaw. Had her answer not satisfied him? She racked her brain for a short list of reasons why she'd ever been interested in him, because the high school version of Jasper had not been this confrontational.

"Yeah, my dad did mention they had found some help with that. Cool. I look forward to seeing what you come up with." He pinned her with a long look.

Miranda sidled up to them and looped her arm around Jasper's waist.

The side eye she offered wasn't lost on Savannah.

"Babe, come on." Miranda tugged Jasper closer. "People want to hang with you."

Jasper's gaze held Savannah's. She refused to look away.

"I'll probably see you around," he said. "Good luck with Wren. She's a handful."

With that, he turned and walked away, letting his new fiancée guide him toward a circle of people they'd gone to high school with.

Wren's cry pierced the air, pulling Savannah's

attention back to Levi. He'd dropped to the ground beside her near the bottom of the slide. The other children had scattered. Levi scooped Wren into his arms and carried her across the yard. Her soiled dress hung limply from Wren's slight body. Savannah's heart pinched at the wounded expression on Levi's face.

What brings you back to town?

Jasper's question replayed in her head as Levi stepped inside the house with Wren. Had she made a terrible mistake coming home? Or was her guilt still wreaking havoc? The art teacher position hadn't been posted yet, but she still held out hope that the school district would make an announcement soon. Then maybe she'd get another chance to start fresh.

He hadn't been this angry with Jasper in a long time. Not since their first year in college, when Jasper had convinced him to finish a project for him during a class final and they'd both gotten in trouble. He'd nearly failed the class until Jasper stepped forward at the last minute and confessed to being the instigator. Man, he loved his twin, but sometimes the guy really aggravated him. Why had Jasper made things so awkward with Savannah?

That was a question he intended to ask, just as soon as he got Wren settled and could catch Jasper alone.

"Come on, Wren. I found some dry clothes for you." He held the little girl's hand as he guided her down the hallway toward the bathroom inside his parents' home. Wren had zipped down the slide a little too fast and landed on her backside in a small muddy puddle at the bottom. The other children playing nearby had laughed, and she'd been crushed. After he'd brought her into the house a few minutes ago, she'd stopped crying, but her tangled hair, muddy dress and hurt feelings had demanded a breather from the party. To be honest, he could use a bit of a time-out himself. Before he said something or did something to Jasper he'd regret later.

"Can I watch TV?" Wren asked softly.

"How about you watch one show, and I'll get you something to eat after you change?"

She pushed a mass of hair out of her eyes and then nodded.

Poor thing. She looked exhausted. Maybe they should just go home. He turned on the light in the bathroom, then handed her the cotton shorts and T-shirt he'd found in his sister's old bedroom. Thankfully, his mom had saved some of their childhood stuff. He made a mental note to pack extra clothes in his backpack the next time they left the house. Not that Wren had come to him with much. Sometimes the fact that she liked to wear the same dress again and again was a blessing in disguise.

He leaned against the wall in the hallway and studied the arrangement of framed pictures hanging beside the bathroom. Most of them featured him, Jasper and their sister, Nyla. A few photos captured Dad's various hunting trips around Alaska and a couple of his grandparents in their younger days. Growing up in a close-knit family who adored the rugged outdoors had always been part of his identity. He'd never questioned it. But lately, the tension that flowed like an undercurrent between him, his father and Jasper made him uneasy.

The doorknob twisted, and Wren emerged, her face still splotchy from crying.

"You look adorable," he said.

She held up her dress. "Dirty again."

Her chin wobbled and he gritted his teeth. *Please, no more tears tonight.* "It's all right. Savannah will understand. We can wash it."

"Okay." She heaved a sigh as she made her way into the family room, then climbed onto the sofa.

After helping Wren find a show to watch on his parents' television, Levi draped one of his mom's well-loved quilts over her legs. "I'll be right back. I'm going to go outside and get us something to eat."

Wren nodded, already craning her neck to see around him.

Levi patted the top of her head, then walked

toward the back door. Before he could get there, Jasper stepped inside. Blocking his exit.

"Dude, what was that?" The words tumbled out before Levi could stop them.

A muscle in Jasper's jaw twitched. "What are you talking about?"

Levi planted his feet wide and linked his arms across his chest. "You confronted Savannah and put us both in an awkward position. Not cool, man."

Irritation flashed in Jasper's eyes. "Awkward, huh? Who's fault is that?"

Levi checked to make sure Wren hadn't popped up off the sofa to listen in on their conversation. Then he stepped closer to his twin and lowered his voice. "What is the matter with you? Why do you care if Savannah is back in town and if we're hanging out?"

"Because I don't want to see you get hurt," Jasper said.

"How is she going to hurt me?"

Jasper scrubbed a hand over his face. "You and Tori didn't break up all that long ago. And—"

"Thanks for the reminder." Levi didn't even try to keep the snark from his voice. "You've already mentioned she's here with someone new as well. Did you give her the same speech about the perils of rebound relationships?"

"I don't really care who Tori's here with. I'm not even sure who invited her, but that's not the point," Jasper said. "You're my brother, and it's not like you to be so impulsive."

"So you're willing to admit that impulsive choices aren't a good idea?"

Jasper's gaze narrowed. "What's that supposed to mean?"

Levi shook his head and tried to walk around him. "Never mind."

Jasper stepped into his path. "No way. You don't get to walk out after making a comment like that. What are you not saying?"

Levi hesitated. "Your proposal to Miranda was kind of sudden. Some might even call it impulsive."

"Is it, now? Or maybe you're jealous because things didn't work out for you and Tori."

Anger flared in his chest, molten hot and looking for an outlet. This was the second time Jasper had accused him of wanting others to share in his misery. Frankly, he was getting a little sick of it.

Thankfully, the back door opened again, and Savannah tried to come in, but the door bumped against Jasper's heel.

"Sorry," she mouthed through the window at Levi.

"Let her in, Jasper," Levi said quietly.

Jasper reluctantly moved out of the way.

Levi motioned for her to enter.

"I'm sorry to interrupt." Her gaze skittered between the two.

"Not a problem. I'm here to grab a sweatshirt for Miranda." Jasper shot Levi another long look before brushing past him and moving toward the stairs.

"I was just on my way back out to get some food and find you," Levi said. "Is everything okay?"

She hesitated. "I'm going to catch a ride home with my sister Juliet. Is Wren all right?"

"Wren's fine." Levi gripped the door with his hand. "But you don't need to leave."

"Oh, I think I do."

He stepped closer. "If this is about what Jasper said, I—"

"It's fine, Levi. Everything's fine. This isn't really my scene." She tried for a smile, but he spotted the hurt swimming in her eyes. Man, he did not like that his family had made her feel unwelcome.

"I'll catch up with you tomorrow."

"Yeah, let's talk soon," he said, but she'd already turned and walked away. He stood in the doorway, watching as she joined her sister, then disappeared around the corner of the house. He sensed the weight of someone watching and surveyed the people standing close by. His gaze collided with Tori's. The edge of her mouth tipped up in a hesitant smile. Levi didn't smile back. Instead, he stepped into the yard and quickly filled a plate of food for himself and Wren to share. He didn't want to give Jasper the satisfaction of being right, but he couldn't quite snuff out his twin's words.

It's not like you to be so impulsive.

Yeah, well, Jasper might call Levi and Savannah spending time together *impulsive*. Levi would rather label it as *kindness*. Savannah hadn't given him any reason to be suspicious. To be honest, he was glad to have her help and her companionship. Especially with Tori still hanging around town. He'd show Jasper and all of Opportunity that Savannah had only the best of intentions.

The next day, Savannah sat at a table beside the window in Riverside Café. *What a gorgeous view*, she mused. Sure, Colorado had rivers and trees and plenty of mountains, but nothing quite like this. People stood on the banks of the King River, the lush green poplar trees forming a canopy over them. In the distance, a swirl of white clouds blanketed the top of Denali like a generous dollop of whipped cream on an ice-cream sundae.

Savannah tapped the end of her colored pencil against her blank sketch pad. Her fingers itched to capture the beauty of her surroundings on the page. Except she needed to focus on her assignment—drawing out her plan for the Carters' parade float. Too bad her thoughts kept wandering to the party last night, her hasty exit with her sister and the tenderness that had lingered in Levi's gaze. He'd been so concerned that he'd even followed up with a late-night text to make sure she was all right. The truth was, Jasper had gotten to her.

Maybe she should just confess to Levi. Tell him why she'd lost her job in Colorado and come home to Opportunity. But that tragic event didn't have anything to do with their current arrangement. Besides, she'd never let anything happen to Wren. And no charges had ever been brought against her, though she'd been tried and shamed in the court of public opinion.

She shook off the negative thoughts before she spiraled into despair and started drawing a pirate ship, complete with an ominous plank that had to be walked. Ever since she'd taken Wren to the park and they'd climbed on the play structure shaped like a boat, she'd toyed with the idea of building a similar float. The café's front door opened, but she refused to look up. Instead, she selected a brown pencil from the array of options in her box and shaded in the stern of the ship. Wow, it felt good to be drawing again, to see what flowed from her fingertips.

"Mind if I join you?"

Levi's familiar voice surprised her. The tip of her pencil broke, and she glanced up at him.

He winced. "Sorry. I didn't mean to startle you."

"No, it's fine. I was just working on a picture."

He cocked his head and leaned in. "That's a nice pirate ship."

"Thanks." She flipped the cover on her sketch book closed.

"You don't have to stop just because I'm here," he said.

"I'm working on ideas for your float. A pirate ship might be too elaborate on a limited budget and short notice."

"Don't be too quick to write off your ideas. We're open to any and all suggestions. You're the professional, remember?" He smiled as he gripped the back of the chair across from her own.

Levi was so thoughtful. How had she not remembered that about him? And why had Tori been so willing to let him go?

Not that their breakup was any of her concern. She dropped the pencil back into its slot in the case. "Did Wren go to the church this morning for Bible school?"

"She did, although it wasn't easy convincing her to try something new."

Savannah wrinkled her nose. "I'm sorry to hear that. Do you still want me to pick her up at one?"

"Yes, please. I'm working from one to nine at the store. If you'll take her back to the house, then my mom will swing by and pick her up around five thirty. Sound good?"

She nodded. Levi had found a spot for Wren at the local church's summer Vacation Bible School program. Four hours was maybe a bit much for a four-year-old, but Levi had told Savannah he wanted Wren to spend some time around other kids in a safe environment. She couldn't argue with him about that, although she expected Wren might be worn out from all the stimulation from singing, making crafts and adjusting to a new set of expectations.

Levi gestured toward her mug, which, sadly, was empty. "Can I get you a refill?"

"Sure. Just regular coffee, please."

"Be right back." He weaved his way through the other tables and across the café. The barista stationed behind the counter smiled and greeted him. Savannah didn't know the woman, but Levi clearly did, because they chatted for a few minutes before he placed his order.

Savannah ran her hand over her collection of pencils, enjoying the sensation of the instruments rolling underneath her fingertips. More details of the pirate ship she'd been sketching unfurled in her imagination. She flipped open the cover of her sketch pad again, then hesitated when the bell on the café's door announced another arrival. And this time, she couldn't help but notice.

Mr. Schubert, the principal at the high school, along with a young woman who followed him inside.

She wore her sleek, platinum blond hair twisted into a perfect bun. Her stylish red-rimmed eyeglasses, open-toed wedges, blue pin-striped blouse and denim skirt weren't the kind of fashionable elements most women in Opportunity wore during the summer.

Definitely not a local.

Several other heads in the café turned. Levi spoke to Mr. Schubert, then shook hands with the stranger. Savannah quickly looked away. No need to get caught gawking.

A few minutes later, Levi returned and carefully set a steaming mug of coffee down in front of her.

"You don't want any cream or sugar?"

"No, this is fine. Thanks."

He claimed the chair across from hers. After setting his own mug between them, his gaze found hers again. "Are you sure I'm not bothering you?"

"No, not at all." She forced a smile but quickly shifted in her chair, unable to resist studying the woman standing beside the principal. "Who is that lady wearing the red glasses?"

Levi hesitated. "Reese, or something. I didn't catch her last name. She's interviewing for a teaching position."

Oh. "At the high school?"

He didn't answer. "So tell me more about this pirate-ship concept. I'm intrigued."

"Please don't change the subject. What does she teach?"

He leaned close. "Don't get upset, but she's a candidate for the art-teacher position."

Her breath hitched. "But the job hasn't even been posted yet."

"Like I said, don't get upset. Or jump to conclusions. It's probably an oversight."

"Or they're not going to post the job because they already have someone in mind," Savannah said, dropping her voice to a whisper.

"The school district can't *not* post a job." Levi reached for his coffee. "That's not legal. Is it?"

"I don't know. But if they're bringing in candidates already, then I don't stand a chance." Savannah's throat tightened as she opened her tote bag and dropped the sketch pad and container of pencils inside.

"Wait." Levi gently clasped her forearm, his fingers warm against her skin. "You're panicking. Don't do that. What's meant to be will be. I'm sure the job will get posted soon, and you'll get to apply."

She wanted to believe him. Really, she did. But the stylish woman was currently laughing like she'd been the principal's best friend for years. That made her panic. Who could blame her?

"Before you rush off, can we talk about what happened last night?"

Abandoning her bag, she slumped back in her chair and forced herself to meet his gaze. "What about last night?"

His eyebrows sailed upward. "You left the party

not long after we got there. Did something happen?"

"You mean, other than your twin brother hassling us and making things super awkward?"

Levi's expression grew stormy. Savannah was taken aback. Was that anger in his eyes directed at Jasper? Did they often fight like this? She couldn't remember them disagreeing much in high school. Maybe they'd put up a united front back then.

"I spoke to Jasper about that." He ran his hand through his hair. "Unfortunately, he doesn't seem to have a problem with the way he behaved. But I do. It wasn't right, and I'm so sorry I even put you in that position."

"I could have stayed home. It's not like you coerced me."

"But it was my idea. Even though this probably sounds petty—to be honest, I really wanted to make Tori jealous."

"I think it worked," Savannah said softly.

He released a short laugh. "Not a chance. She doesn't care one bit anymore."

"That can't be true. I mean, you were engaged, right? Surely she still has feelings for you."

"Engaged doesn't mean anything if a person can't be honest about their hopes and dreams," Levi said bitterly.

Oh no. Her stomach twisted as guilt slithered in. "Levi, I…"

She trailed off when he reached out and took

her hand. "Thank you for going along with my stupid plan. If you want out now, I won't blame you."

Savannah looked into his eyes, seeing the pain and vulnerability lurking beneath the surface. She squeezed his hand tightly. "I'm not going anywhere."

Chapter Five

Savannah needed to come up with something for the parade float. Quickly. Only he hadn't given her much to work with. Now that he'd seen her pirate-ship sketch, he felt guilty for roping her into helping them. She was capable of producing something spectacular, but he knew Dad and Jasper weren't receptive to splurging on supplies. He'd gently introduced the idea at the store yesterday afternoon, and they'd both shut him down. Funny how they wanted a great float that attracted customers and generated more business but didn't want to spend much money to make it happen.

"Come on, Wren. This way." With Wren's sticky hand clasped in his, Levi led the way across the field on his grandparents' property.

"What is this place?" Wren asked, using her other hand to shove her hair out of her eyes.

Her cheeks had red sticky stuff on them, evidence of the lollipop he'd let her enjoy on the ride over from the store. She'd been a real trouper about going to Vacation Bible School. When he'd picked her up at the church that afternoon, she'd begged him to take her to the park instead of back to the store. He already hated disappointing her. Thankfully, the promise of coming here and seeing Savannah had cheered her up. Still, he hadn't been able to tell her no when she'd asked for the lollipop from the candy section near the store's cash register.

"This is my grandparents' backyard," Levi said. "Savannah is working on a special project for a parade. We're keeping everything she needs in the old barn."

Although, it wasn't a barn at all. More like a shed to store his grandfather's vintage classic pickup truck. That and the trailer were the only two things he could say for sure would work for the parade float.

"Big yard," Wren said.

Levi chuckled. "Yeah, it is pretty big. Jasper and my sister and I have had a lot of fun back here over the years."

A pair of swallows chirped as they flitted past, and the familiar loamy scent of the soil in his grandparents' garden nearby greeted him. Grandma loved growing produce she could display at the state fair in Palmer later in the summer. She'd been known to bring home the prize for the biggest cabbage a time or two.

"What do you play here?" Wren stumbled over the uneven ground. Levi squeezed her hand to keep her upright, then slowed his steps. He eyed the neglected fort in the trees on the other side of the barn and the three huge tires Grandpa had probably salvaged from a piece of heavy equipment ages ago. Levi and Jasper had hidden in those and played their own made-up version of hide-and-seek countless times with the neighbor kids who lived across the road. His heart pinched at all the good memories.

Could he and Jasper ever get back to that place in their relationship? Where they had fun, made memories and didn't care about one-upping each other?

"Lee-by?" Wren stared up at him, pulling him back to the present. "What games are here?"

"Oh, we played tag, hide-and-seek, kick the can…"

Wren giggled. "Kick the *can*? What's that?"

Despite his melancholy thoughts, Levi couldn't help but smile at Wren's infectious laughter. "We'll have to teach you sometime. It's like tag, hide-and-seek and capture the flag all mixed together."

She eyed him as if he'd spoken a foreign language.

"Let's unlock this door. Savannah will be here in a few minutes." He stopped in front of the barn, let go of Wren's hand and pulled the key from his pocket.

Wren's brow furrowed. She tentatively reached

out and touched the two-by-four-foot wood slab blocking the barn's door. "What's this?"

"We keep a lock on the door and also that piece of wood to keep it shut in case the wind blows extra hard or an animal tries to get inside." Levi slid the key into the padlock. The metal bar sprang open after an easy twist.

"No animals allowed?"

He removed the lock and the piece of wood, then carefully slid the broad door open. "My grandparents have two dogs and three cats. Mostly, they live outside. Only the truck, the trailer and some tools stay here."

Dust particles floating in the air caught the late-afternoon sunlight. Wren's face wrinkled; then she sneezed.

"Bless you." Levi pocketed his key and gestured toward the red truck. "See? My grandfather's truck and trailer."

"Can we ride now?"

"Not today. We have to help Savannah get ready for the parade."

She tilted her head to one side. "What's a parade?"

"You'll see. It's like a big party that goes right through town. Everybody lines up to watch, some people who are in the parade will throw candy and—"

"Candy." The word left her lips on a gasp, and her eyes grew wide. "Can I have some?"

Levi turned and squinted in the semidarkness, searching for the battery-powered lantern Grandpa usually left inside the barn. "When it's time, yes, you may."

"When is the parade? Today?"

"No." Levi spotted the lantern, picked it up and turned the knob. The bulbs flickered on. "It's on the Fourth of July."

"Is that tomorrow?"

Oh brother. Levi tried not to show his impatience. "It's in about fifteen wake-ups."

A measurement of time he'd learned from one of his friends with kids. Sleeping and waking up made sense when terms like *afternoon, next week* and *next month* didn't seem to compute. At least for Wren.

"It's gonna rain tomorrow." She hopped from one foot to the next, kicking up dust in the barn's doorway. "I'm glad the party thingy isn't then."

"Yeah, me too." Levi smiled. "How do you know about tomorrow's weather?"

"The rain-cloud sign on TV, silly."

Ah, that's right. He'd had the news on for a few minutes before breakfast—until he realized the leading stories were not suitable for kids. Good thing he'd shut it off right after the weather forecast.

A squirrel darted in, then darted right back out. The sun warmed his back as he stood facing the truck and tried to envision a clever design for the float. Savannah's pirate-ship sketch had been epic, but he was afraid to ask what she'd need to pull that off. The muffled hum of a vehicle moving closer quickened his steps as Wren turned and trotted toward the car.

"Wren, wait." He had to jog to catch her before she ran across the field alone.

The determined little girl ignored him.

Thankfully, he recognized Savannah behind the wheel of the white sedan. She'd slowed to nearly a crawl, then eased to a stop and parked next to his grandparents' house.

"Sabby!" Wren yelled, her little fist knocking on the driver's-side window.

"Wren, you can't run at people's cars like that." Levi didn't want to scold her, but that was exactly the kind of dangerous behavior that sent him spiraling into a panic.

Savannah climbed out of the vehicle. Uncertainty flashed in her eyes as she looked between Wren and Levi. "Is everything okay?"

"Yep." Wren grabbed Savannah's hand and tugged her to the barn. "Come see the truck."

"Wait." Levi stepped in front of them. "Wren, we have to talk about what just happened."

Wren pooched out her lower lip and avoided eye contact.

Savannah stood still, her hand captured between both of Wren's. Her expression was filled with empathy.

Levi slowly sank down to the little girl's eye level. "Pumpkin, I need you to know how important it is that you not run toward moving cars. Ever."

"But I'm just happy," Wren whispered.

"I know. Me too. Being with Savannah is one of my favorite things."

Uh-oh. The words had slipped out before he could give them careful thought. Savannah's breath hitched. He kept his gaze trained on Wren.

"I'm sorry, Lee-by." Wren's chin wobbled. "I'll be good."

Oh, this kid. Her pitiful attempts to win his favor speared him every time.

"I know you will." He reached out and cupped her shoulder gently with his hand. "It's my job to keep you safe, and I don't want you to get hurt, because I care about you."

She nodded but still wouldn't look at him. He dragged his gaze to meet Savannah's, already questioning his methods and silently seeking her wisdom.

"It's fine," Savannah mouthed without making any sound.

Let it go. Message delivered. He stood and angled his head toward the barn. "We'd better go show Savannah the truck."

Savannah grinned, and they fell into step beside each other. "How are your grandparents?"

"They're doing well." Levi reached for Wren's

hand and guided her around a mud puddle. "Enjoying retirement. They're over at my aunt and uncle's place for dinner."

Wren tugged free and ran ahead. Levi slowed his steps, waiting for her to turn and dash back toward the puddle. At the last second, she got distracted by a butterfly fluttering outside the barn's door. Another load of mud-splattered laundry avoided. For now.

"That's a pretty one, isn't it, Wren?" Savannah pointed toward the black-and-yellow insect as it dipped toward the blooming flowers in the wood planters nearby.

"So pretty," Wren whispered.

Inside the barn, Levi found another battery-powered lamp and set it near the back of the truck. Savannah plopped her bag on the hood but didn't pull out her sketch pad. Instead, she gave Wren her full attention as the little girl delivered a detailed rundown of her activities. Part of him was annoyed that she had hardly mentioned any of it to him, but he had to admit, she and Savannah were fun to watch. They had such an easy way together. No stress. No tension. Savannah knew just what to say—and the right questions to ask to get Wren to share more details. He could get used to this, the three of them hanging out together. Not that he could get attached. Savannah hadn't locked down a full-time job, and he had no idea how long Wren would be with him.

"So does the truck still run?" Savannah braced her hands on her hips.

"My uncle and my grandfather said they start it every now and then and take it for a spin. The main thing will be figuring out what it's going to pull."

Savannah pointed toward her bag. "I brought my sketch pad. The pirate-ship idea got elaborate too quickly. But no worries because I have a backup plan."

"I am worried about getting the right materials," Levi said. "Will you be able to get what you need in time?"

"We'll have to get creative." Her eyes sparkled as she smiled, and his heart thrummed in his chest.

"I need to take some measurements," she said.

"There's probably a tape measure right over here." Levi crossed over to the dusty workbench in the corner of the barn.

"Can I help?" Wren asked.

"Of course," Savannah said.

Levi brought Savannah the measuring tape and tried not to stare as she circled the truck, somehow answering all Wren's questions without getting flustered.

The next time he and Savannah were alone, he'd ask for pointers on how to relax with Wren instead of behaving like a lifeguard. Constantly staying on high alert was exhausting. Except he didn't know how to dial it back. He'd never forgive himself if anything happened to her.

Was she doing the right thing? After meeting Levi and Wren at the barn the other day, Savannah still wondered if applying for a job here in Opportunity was the best choice. There were so many memories and now, so many complications. Hopefully this bike trip with her siblings would clear her head.

"Wyatt Morgan, why do you think this is fun?" Juliet abandoned her bike beside the trail, then sagged onto the picnic table bench with a dramatic groan.

Grinning, Wyatt eased to a stop. "It's good for you, sis."

Savannah climbed off her bike, propped it with the kickstand and then unbuckled her helmet.

Chest heaving, Juliet narrowed her gaze. "Why aren't you as miserable as me?"

Savannah hesitated. She and her ex-boyfriend had often hiked and ridden their bikes in Colorado. But she didn't want to think about him now. "Maybe try riding your bike more than once every five years."

Juliet plucked her water bottle from her knapsack. "Maybe some of us prefer water aerobics."

Savannah couldn't stop a laugh. Oh, how she'd missed bantering with her brother and sisters. She retrieved her own water bottle, along with three energy bars. She offered them to Wyatt and Juliet.

"No, thanks." Juliet eyed the snack's wrapper. "I'm good."

"I brought my own," Wyatt said.

"All right." Savannah shrugged, tore one corner off the wrapper and took a bite of the peanut butter–chocolate concoction. It wasn't bad. But not as tasty as she'd hoped.

Hayley rolled up on her bike, sweaty and out of breath. "This was so not a good idea."

"Savvy wanted to do some sibling bonding," Juliet said, her water bottle crinkling in her hand.

"I thought we'd make s'mores around the campfire or something." Hayley swiped her forearm across her flushed cheeks. "How does riding a bike uphill on a hot day help us bond?"

Wyatt stood at the edge of the trail. "Don't you think this view is worth all the effort?" He swept his hand around him in a wide circle.

"That's a good point," Savannah said. The mountain, only partially obstructed by clouds, stood like a regal lady swathed in robes of purple and green and blue, and crowned with bright white yet-to-melt snow. Brilliant purple and pink wildflowers cascaded across the lower elevations, contrasted by verdant green forests. Colorado had plenty of tall peaks, but there was nothing quite like a view of Denali on a gorgeous summer day.

Hayley climbed on top of the picnic table and lay on her back. "What's on your mind?"

Savannah's heart squeezed. "I wanted to hang out with you guys, that's all. Seems like everybody's busy with work and stuff."

Okay, so maybe she was chickening out a little. She'd planned to tell her siblings the reason why she'd had to come home. But now that didn't feel right. What would she gain from burdening them with her secret?

"Some of us are busy spending quality time with Levi Carter," Juliet teased, nudging Savannah's shoulder.

"It's not what you think." Savannah looked away, the snack turning to cardboard in her mouth.

"People are talking," Hayley said. "Sounds like you two are having a good time together."

"Yeah, what's going on there?" Frowning, Wyatt turned toward the picnic table and linked his muscular arms across his chest. "Are you sure dating him is a good idea?"

"You sound like Jasper," Savannah said.

"Well, Jasper and I aren't really friends, and we haven't been discussing your personal life. But you did just get here," Wyatt said. "I'm surprised you've started dating someone so soon."

"Yeah, about that," Savannah said. "Levi asked me to help him out. I don't know the details, but Tori pretty much crushed him when she ended their engagement."

"Yeah, because she's still here," Hayley said. "Thought she was moving to Massachusetts or something."

"Iowa, for dental school," Juliet clarified. "But not until August."

"Then why is she hanging around with the guy who works at the hotel if she's planning to move?" Hayley sat up and tucked her knees under her chin.

"That's a question we're all asking," Savannah said.

"Not all of us," Wyatt said. "I don't care—at least, not about Tori. But I do care about you, Savvy. And I don't want you to get hurt."

The look of concern on his face gave her pause. It was quite similar to the look he'd given her when they'd come home from the airport. "It's going to be fine, Wyatt."

Wasn't it? She'd convinced herself that Levi had a sound plan—to let them both enjoy reunion activities without being besieged by eager matchmakers or a pity party for Levi, but now Wyatt's questions burrowed under her skin and brought all the doubt right back to the surface.

Hayley dug into Juliet's bag, then pulled out a package of peanut butter M&M's. "Are you going to all the class reunion activities together?"

Savannah winced. "Yes. Sort of."

Hayley pinned her with a long look. "What are you not telling us?"

"I agreed to be Levi's fake date."

A muscle in Wyatt's cheek twitched. "I sure hope you're joking."

"Oh, this is going to be fun." Juliet clapped her hands together. "That's so romantic."

"And so not like you," Hayley added. "He must have been so persuasive."

"Back to the Tori thing," Savannah said. "She crushed him. It's so obvious when he talks about her that he's not over her. And I don't think she's over him."

"She kept a close watch on the two of you at the engagement party." Juliet held out her palm for Hayley to share her candy. "Which is so weird because she didn't have to be there."

"Tori has known Jasper a long time, and she was about to be his sister-in-law," Savannah said. "Besides, the Carters invited almost the entire town."

"Still, it was awkward," Juliet said. "I'm glad we made a quick exit."

"I'm glad I didn't go at all." Wyatt got back on his bike. "Are you girls ready to head home?"

"Wow, you are in a mood today." Savannah frowned at him. "Do you need to go for a longer bike ride? Get those endorphins going?"

"I'd love to keep going. I only stopped because you said you were tired." He buckled his helmet strap under his chin. "Ready when you are."

Savannah pushed to her feet. "I appreciate your

concern about my agreement with Levi. Since I haven't kept in touch with my classmates, it will be nice to have someone to go to the events with."

Hayley put the leftover candy back in Juliet's knapsack. "What about your bestie, Grace?"

"She's flying in from California later this week. Her boss at the bank only approved a week of vacation, so she couldn't take time off from work to attend every single event."

"Hope she makes it for the softball game." Juliet returned to her bike. "You all need a lot of people to field a team."

"Ugh. No, thank you." Savannah returned to her bike. "Softball is so not my thing."

"Well, it's still Opportunity's thing." Wyatt took a sip from his water bottle, then put it back in the holder on his bike. "The Summer Solstice Softball Tournament is the highlight of the summer around here."

"It doesn't have to be," Savannah said. "There's bike riding, white water rafting and trails to hike. Someone is planning a get-together at a former teacher's house—plus, there's the formal dance at the hotel."

"People still take their softball very seriously," Juliet said. "Especially when there's no darkness to contend with and they can play all night if they want."

Savannah blew out a long breath. "I will not be

participating in a midnight softball game under any circumstances."

"You should go and support your class." Hayley got back on her bike. "Or offer to help serve hamburgers and hot dogs afterward?"

"Maybe they'll let me stand in the outfield and daydream, just like I did in high school. What could possibly go wrong?"

As they rode their bikes back down the hill toward home, the sunlight on her back warming her skin, the weight of doubt settled in her chest. She tried not to think too much about what her siblings had said. But they loved her and knew her best, so it wasn't easy to dismiss their concerns. Was Wyatt right? Had she made a mistake by agreeing to be Levi's fake girlfriend?

On Thursday morning, Levi stood behind the counter at the store, his phone pressed to his ear. "What do you mean, Wren can't stay? We have two more days of Vacation Bible School."

"I understand your frustration," Mrs. Horvath said calmly. "But Wren's behavior has become increasingly disruptive, and her small-group leader has no other choice but to ask her to leave."

"So you think the solution to the teenager not being able to handle the four-year-olds is to blame the kid? Maybe you should just get a new small-group leader."

"That won't help with Wren's situation," she said.

Anger boiled in his chest. "What do you mean by 'situation'?"

"We've caught her stealing bags of peanut butter crackers from the snack closet. Twice."

"That doesn't seem like something that should be punished. She's a young child who has faced hunger and poverty. Instead of taking her out of the program, why don't we try to talk to her?"

"We have made our expectations clear, Mr. Carter." Mrs. Horvath's tone had turned frigid. "Wren chose to disobey. Stealing isn't allowed. It could be harmful to the other children if they see her act this way."

"Mrs. Horvath, I think we could show some mercy here. This is a summer camp, not a full-day school."

"I'm not looking to argue with you."

Dark spots floated before his eyes. "So, what's the policy? Is *any* misbehaving child being removed from VBS or only Wren?"

"That's none of your concern," she said. "You need to get here in the next fifteen minutes and take Wren with you."

"Are you saying that if I don't come, you'll call the police?"

"I'm contacting everyone on your emergency-contact list until someone retrieves the child. If no one is willing or able to come, I'll have to inform the authorities."

"It's strange that a church wouldn't provide a

safe haven for young kids who are having difficulties. Isn't that the point of Vacation Bible School?"

"Our VBS has two goals, which we make clear to our parents and guardians—one is to provide a healthy, wholesome environment for the kids who attend, and the other is to provide teens with a similar experience working with the children. We've tried very hard to balance those goals. In Wren's case, she's made it too difficult for our teen group leaders. Maybe when she's older, she'll be fine. There are special activities planned for the rest of the week, and we'd need extra volunteers to keep an eye on Wren. That's simply not feasible. I'll see you in a few minutes."

She hung up the phone.

He was stunned. Had that just happened?

"Is everything all right?" Jasper asked, passing a stack of hangers to Miranda from across the counter. They had been tagging and organizing a new shipment of women's clothing in the store. Dad stood near the clothing rack, updating the inventory electronically.

Levi was too angry about the phone call he'd just received to even think about why Miranda was helping out in the store today. She definitely wasn't being paid. "Mrs. Horvath called from church. She's kicking Wren out of Vacation Bible School," he said.

Miranda gasped. "That's terrible. Isn't Wren, like, three or something?"

"Four, actually," Levi said sadly. "And thank you for your concern. It really is horrible."

"Is she in trouble?" Jasper asked, collapsing the now-empty cardboard box and tucking it away.

"Apparently, according to Mrs. Horvath, she's stealing peanut butter crackers and not following the rules," he said with a hint of exasperation. "The teenager assigned to Wren's class can't handle her. I have to go get her right away."

Dad shut the electronic tablet he was holding. "Right now? Vacation Bible School ends tomorrow. Can't they keep her there for just one more day?"

Levi shoved his phone into his pocket. "She's disrupting everything so much that they can't cope. They gave me fifteen minutes' notice."

Dad shook his head in disbelief. "I'll need to discuss this with Pastor Blanchett on Sunday. I doubt he's in favor of removing kids from VBS."

"Thanks for your input, Dad, but Mrs. Horvath seems to think she's following church policies and procedures." Blood pounded in his head. What happened to having grace and compassion when a kid messed up?

Outside, a delivery truck's brakes hissed, and then the methodical *beep, beep, beep* ensued as it backed up to the store.

"Let me and Miranda go get her," Jasper suggested.

"What will you do with her?" Levi asked.

"Take her fishing, like Dad used to do with me when I messed up in school."

Levi glanced at their father. "Wait, you really did that? Does Mom know?"

Dad waved his hand in dismissal. "That was a long time ago. Best not to bring it up again."

Levi turned back to Jasper. "Make sure she doesn't run off. Wren isn't very patient."

Jasper chuckled at his brother's concern. "It'll be fun. If she can't stand still and fish, we'll let her wander around for a bit. Want to go fishing, babe?" he asked Miranda, nudging her shoulder gently.

Miranda hung up the last shirt on the rack and put on a brave face. "Sure thing. I haven't done that since I was eight, though—you may need to give me some pointers."

"You need to have Wren back by lunchtime. She gets cranky when she misses a meal." Levi dragged his hand over his face. He really needed to make sure she took a decent nap today too. Maybe that's why she was having a hard time listening and paying attention to the rules.

"We should take her out somewhere after fishing, like the Sluice Box or Gunnar's. Don't you think?" Jasper asked.

Levi didn't bother to hide his skepticism. "Are you sure? We're talking about an energetic four-year-old here. Do you think you can handle it?"

Miranda nodded confidently in response, although there seemed to be a hint of uncertainty on her face.

"Just one more thing," Levi said.

"Keep her away from the river?"

"Yes, that too. And…you cannot post any pictures of her online."

Irritation flashed in Jasper's eyes. "Why would we be posting someone else's child's pictures on the internet?"

Levi felt awful for even bringing it up, but he had to let them know. "It's a rule I'm legally obligated to follow as her foster parent. I can't—"

"Yeah, yeah, no need to explain. Feed her, keep her dry and don't let her go fishing without supervision. Anything else?"

He winced at Jasper's impatience. They really were trying to help. Levi sighed, then met his twin's gaze. "Thank you guys so much for taking this on. It means a lot."

"Let's get going, then, babe." Miranda took Jasper's hand, and they left the store.

"You'll need a photo ID when you pick Wren up," Levi called after them. Jasper raised his hand in response before heading out.

His dad patted Levi on the shoulder. "Wren is going to be okay. They'll make sure she stays alive."

"I know." Levi stared after his brother and Miranda as they walked hand in hand toward Jasper's car in the parking lot. "They're helping me out when I'm in a bind. I should probably be more grateful." He snatched up the stack of cardboard Jasper had left behind and carted it to the back of the store, frustrated with himself for being so hard on his brother lately.

He needed to go fishing or something to blow off steam because he had some harsh words ready for Mrs. Horvath. How could she do something like that, knowing Wren had already been through so much?

Chapter Six

She'd stay for an hour. Two at the most. Just long enough to say hello to everyone, and if things went well, eat dinner. Quickly. Savannah grabbed her purse and the bouquet of wildflowers she'd tucked into a mason jar, then eased out of Wyatt's truck. Levi and Wren were supposed to meet her here, although he'd sent a text before she'd left the house that they were running late. Looping her purse strap over her shoulder, she eyed Mr. Jackson's front door. Her high school English teacher had owned this gorgeous home overlooking the Poplar River for as long as she could remember. He and his wife had hosted dozens of events here. An especially sweet memory came rushing back. Suddenly, she was fifteen again, celebrating her team's victory at the academic decathlon.

They'd been so excited when they'd come from behind and upset that incredible team from Kenai, even though Candace and her crowd had teased them relentlessly for being total nerds. The familiar anxiety crawled across her skin. She reached for the truck's door handle.

No. Don't be a coward.

Ten years had passed. Surely they could all catch up with one another and behave like adults.

A water balloon sailed over her head and crashed onto the gravel behind her with an obnoxious splat. She squealed as cold water sprayed the back of her legs.

"Oops. Sorry," a deep male voice called out. "That one got out of hand."

Robert, who'd grown up living down the road from her, jogged across the Jacksons' front lawn.

She shook her head, unable to hold back a smile. "You guys didn't waste any time pulling a prank, did you?"

"It was Mr. Jackson's idea." Robert slung an arm around her shoulders and pulled her in for a side hug. "He wanted us to make sure his new water balloon slingshot worked. He needs it for the parade."

Savannah grimaced. "I don't even want to know why he needs a water balloon slingshot at the parade."

"If you go, steer clear of his float. He volunteered to help with the student council this year." Robert pulled back and gave her a friendly once-over. "How've you been, Savannah? Good to see you again."

"It's good to see you too, Robert." She fell in

step beside him. "I hear you and your wife are expecting. Congratulations."

He grinned again. "Thanks. I can hardly wait to meet the little guy. Come on, the party's just getting started. We're hanging out back here."

Their shoes crunched under the gravel as they rounded the side of the house. The aroma of citronella from the tiki torches staked throughout the yard permeated the air. Laughter wafted toward her. She stopped at the edge of the lush green lawn. Robert kept walking, already encouraging a group of three to join him for badminton. Two couples sat at the table under the umbrella on the patio, and a dozen other people stood in clusters around the gorgeous backyard.

Through the trees, the river flowed gently, burbling along behind the property.

"Savannah! I heard you were here, but I had to see you with my own eyes to believe it." Mr. Jackson strode toward her, his long legs making short work of the distance between them. In gray cargo shorts and a rumpled purple T-shirt, he didn't look much different than the young guys milling about. More gray in his brown hair, maybe, and the laugh lines around his eyes had deepened. His same easy smile instantly made her feel welcome.

"Hi, Mr. Jackson." She offered the small glass jar with the flowers inside. "These are for you and Mrs. Jackson."

He carefully accepted the jar. "You didn't have to do that."

"You didn't have to host," she said. "Thank you for inviting us all over. Do you have a party for every class reunion?"

"Not every class. We're thrilled to see you guys again. This is quite a yardful of wonderful humans." Mr. Jackson glanced around, then faced her again. "Welcome home, by the way. How've you been?"

An unexpected tightness made her throat ache. "Yeah, um, thanks. I'm good. Really good."

Mostly.

"Glad to hear it." He clapped her on the shoulder. "Let me run these inside. Go ahead and grab a seat, or get a soda or whatever. We'll visit the taco bar shortly, then get on with the evening's festivities."

Oh no. "And what would those be?"

He laughed, walking backward across the lawn. "The three-legged race is back by popular demand."

She didn't bother to hide her disappointed expression.

"Don't worry. There'll be a rousing game of Pictionary and trivia later on."

"Great." She gave him a thumbs-up. "That I can handle."

After setting her purse on a canvas chair nearby, she crossed over to the coolers lined up near the garage and chose a can of soda. From her vantage point, she looked around, assessing the rest of the guests. Jasper and Miranda stood near the badminton game, speaking with Candace and the guy Savannah assumed was Candace's husband.

They didn't make eye contact, and frankly she didn't have the courage to initiate conversation. Everyone else had paired off or were standing in tight circles. Maybe she should go inside and offer to help Mrs. Jackson with the food. Or text one of her sisters and beg them to stage a faux emergency so she could leave.

As she claimed her seat, then reached inside her purse to find her phone, Levi strode across the lawn, holding Wren's hand.

Wren's eyes lit up when she spotted her. "Sabby."

Savannah tucked her drink into the chair's cupholder and spread her arms wide. Wren tugged her hand free from Levi's and ran toward Savannah.

"Hi, sweet girl." She pulled Wren onto her lap, then exchanged glances with Levi. "I'm so glad you're both here."

Understanding dawned in his eyes. "Tough crowd?"

Savannah shifted Wren on her lap and chose her words carefully. "I thought I'd know more people here, that's all."

"I'm sorry we're a little bit late." He tipped his head toward Wren. "Slight wardrobe malfunction."

Savannah surveyed the little girl's outfit. She had on a pair of jeans with a slight flare at the cuffs and a mint green sweatshirt with a hot-pink-and-white daisy printed on the front. "This is a super-cute outfit. What happened?"

Levi pulled up a chair next to hers. "When I told her the mosquitoes might be an issue, she wanted to wear her sweatshirt over her princess dress. We compromised with jeans and the sweatshirt."

"Good call." Savannah gently tugged on a strand of Wren's hair. "You'll be much happier with fewer bug bites."

Wren twisted around to face her. "Can you make my hair into a pony? 'Cause Lee-by can't."

"Hey, now." Levi gave them both the side eye. "It's not that I *can't*. We lacked the necessary supplies."

Savannah tried her best to conceal her amusement. "Such as?"

"A hair thingy," Wren said.

"And a positive attitude," Levi added quietly.

If Wren heard the comment about attitude, she must've decided to ignore it. "Will you, Sabby? Make me a pony?"

Wren's hopeful expression and her word choice for the classic hairstyle sent Savannah reaching for her purse. "Absolutely. I bet I have an extra hair thingy in here."

Sensing the curious looks from their classmates

at this oh-so-domestic arrangement, Savannah's fingers trembled as she carefully freed some of the tangles. A few minutes later, she'd secured Wren's hair in a high ponytail with the pink elastic band she'd found in the depths of her purse.

"There." Savannah patted Wren's shoulder. "A pony. Just for you."

"Can I see?" Wren wriggled off her lap. "Where's the bathroom?"

"I'll take you." Savannah stood, then glanced back at Levi. "We'll be back soon."

Something that resembled appreciation flickered in his eyes. Her cheeks warmed under his gaze. *All pretend, remember?*

She took Wren's hand in her own and led her toward the Jacksons' back door. People would stare and probably speculate. But wasn't that what Levi wanted? For the word to get back to Tori that he'd happily moved on?

Levi had never wanted to win a three-legged race so badly in his life. Yet with Savvy's leg tied to his and her arm looped around his waist, he was tempted to go extra slow, stay at the back of the pack and enjoy the warmth of her beside him, the scent of her shampoo or lotion or something— floral and sweet—teasing his senses.

He could tell by the tightness in her jaw and her furtive glances that she'd rather be anywhere else than here right now. Not that he could blame her.

Since he and Wren had arrived in the Jacksons' backyard, their classmates had not been as fun to hang out with as he'd hoped they'd be. Maybe he was too optimistic. Or maybe he'd been so focused on his relationship with Tori that he hadn't bothered to pay attention to the lack of meaningful conversation among some of his former classmates, how the casual small talk never segued to genuine interest in one another's lives. Sure, he socialized from time to time with his childhood friends, and several of them came in the store occasionally. He'd describe those encounters as friendly. But he hadn't made much effort to stay truly connected to the guys he'd grown up with.

If he'd had a strong network beyond Tori and his parents, would fostering Wren be easier? Guilt nipped at him like a stealthy fox on the prowl.

The first heat of the race stumbled across the makeshift finish line on the Jacksons' front lawn, then collapsed in a heap of laughter and limbs. Candace and her husband quickly claimed victory.

"Of course," Savvy said, heaving a deep sigh.

"This race is just getting started." He nudged her gently with his shoulder. "They haven't seen what we're about to bring."

She rolled her eyes but didn't say anything.

Candace and her husband pushed to their feet, hollering and exchanging high fives. Yeah, he definitely wanted to beat them both. Candace's husband was a decent guy, but Candace had overplayed her cards one too many times. And he hadn't forgotten about how she'd spoken to Savvy in the store when Savvy had first come back to Opportunity. The woman couldn't be trusted.

Wren sat on the front-porch steps, eating another cheese quesadilla under Mrs. Jackson's watchful eye. Which meant Levi could focus his full attention on Savannah.

Man, he really wanted to kiss her. Which was absurd because this whole relationship thing was supposed to be fake. Tori hadn't broken up with him all that long ago.

Savannah had only been home for about a week.

He'd noted the skeptical glances. A few whispers behind hands when Savannah fixed Wren's hair before dinner. He'd never been able to hide so much as an ear infection or a common cold in this town, much less pull off pretending to date Savvy in the wake of his crushing breakup. But that wouldn't stop him from trying. And his attraction to the beautiful redhead whose leg was currently tied to his seemed oh so very real.

He cleared his throat and tried to focus. "What's your strategy here?"

She wrinkled her nose. "To not die of embarrassment."

"Oh, come on. That's a little negative, don't you think? This is supposed to be fun."

The edges of her lips twitched. "Perhaps. Just keeping it real, though."

"My objective is to win. Yours is to avoid crushing embarrassment. How can we work together to achieve a common goal?"

She stared up at him. "Wow, Levi Carter. You might have a promising career in school administration, because that was brilliant."

It was his turn to smile. "I have absolutely no interest in being a principal or a teacher. Although, I wouldn't mind being a referee."

"That does look fun. You'd look handsome in stripes."

His heart kicked against his ribs.

"Sorry." Her cheeks flushed, and her gaze skittered away. "I don't know why I said that. You'd be a great referee."

Buoyed by her unexpected compliment, he stood taller. "A lifetime of trying to keep Jasper from cheating has taught me a few things."

"Oh, there's a lot to unpack there."

"You have no idea. Come on, we need to get to the starting line." They worked their way to where the other participants had lined up to race. A cool breeze blew a lock of her hair against his cheek. His fingers itched to tuck it back into place. Ah, there he went. Mesmerized again.

He sensed someone watching them and looked over to where Candace and her husband stood, their legs roped together. Not far away, something indecipherable flickered in Candace's features. The hair on the back of Levi's neck stood on end.

Candace could always be counted on to uncover and keep up with anything interesting happening within a fifty-mile radius of Opportunity. But this time, he did not want to be the source of her curiosity. The woman was the ultimate pot stirrer. Lately, he'd wondered if she'd somehow influenced Tori's decision to abruptly end their engagement. He didn't have proof, so he wasn't about to lob any accusations publicly, and Tori's decision to become a dentist did seem genuine. But Tori had spent quite a bit of time with Candace in the last year, and they'd gone out of town for a long weekend right before Tori broke up with him. Except now, when he turned the notion over in his mind, he felt jealous and petty.

The kind of feelings he'd rather escape.

His eyes drifted back to Savvy's face. The freckles sprinkled across the bridge of her nose, her full pink lips... It wouldn't take much to tip her chin up with one finger and—

"Okay, here's the deal. Our strategy is a come-from-behind victory."

"What?"

Savvy eyed him. "You said you wanted my strategy. I say we go for a come-from-behind victory."

"So try to lose and then don't."

Two ridges appeared in her smooth brow. "Well, not *try* to lose, exactly—but no one's expecting us to win, so how can we pull off an upset?"

He squeezed her shoulder with his hand. "Good plan. I like the way you think."

Maybe they could win this thing.

"Come on, Lee-by and Sabby," Wren cheered from her perch on the steps. She'd obviously found her way to the chips, because she was holding a small bag of Fritos in one hand.

A sigh escaped.

Savvy looked up at him again. "Are you good?"

"Yeah. I mean, she's eating the chips instead of stuffing them in her pocket, so that's a win. Sort of. Do you think I'll ever get her to eat a healthy meal? She only wanted chips and quesadillas for dinner."

"Well, to be fair, they served us tacos from a taco bar. That's a lot of textures to deal with," Savvy said.

"She can handle a corn chip, but she can't handle ground beef and tomatoes inside a crunchy shell?"

"Listen, my love for tacos knows no bounds, but I'm just saying, for some kids, food with a lot of textures can be tough to deal with."

"I should only serve her smooth things?"

Savvy took an awkward step forward, forcing him to follow her closer to the makeshift starting line as Mr. Jackson motioned for them to get ready to race. "Try it. See what happens."

"Will that stop the hoarding?"

She offered a gentle shrug. "I have no idea. Not my area of expertise. But one of my sisters would only eat smooth foods. That's how she survived childhood."

"Now we're getting to the good stuff. Come on, spill all the juicy Morgan-family secrets."

She flinched.

Oh no. What had he done?

Her expression hardened. "Let's focus. The race is about to start."

"Savvy, I didn't—"

"Next heat, please. Savvy, Levi, Robert, Gwen, Calista and Jason," Mr. Jackson called out. "You're up."

A caution flag flapped in his mind. He'd obviously said something to aggravate her, but what? He'd been so impressed by her suggestions. Maybe she thought he'd been mocking her or her family. That hardly seemed realistic. He loved her sisters, and Wyatt too. Her whole family was amazing. He'd have to circle back to this conversation, because the last thing he wanted to do was hurt her.

"On my count, this heat will begin," Mr. Jackson shouted.

"Wow, he's making this sound very official," Savvy murmured as they stood beside Jason and Calista.

Levi flashed her a confident smile. "We've got this."

Her gaze skittered away. Again. But she did tighten her hold around his waist.

Mr. Jackson cupped his hands around his mouth

and projected his voice over the chatter. "On your mark… Get set… Go!"

Adrenaline surged through his veins. He pulled her closer as they half stumbled, half trotted across the yard. Their classmates cheered and clapped, urging each of the three couples to hustle.

For a few glorious seconds, they claimed the lead. "C'mon, Savvy. We're so close."

"I'm trying," she insisted, her words mingling with her nervous laughter.

But when they were a few strides short of the finish line, Jason and Calista blew past them, winning the heat.

He and Savvy crossed in second place. They wouldn't move on to the final round.

She quickly untied the bandannas securing their legs, then straightened and offered him a smile that didn't quite reach her eyes. "Good job."

Disappointment settled low in his gut. "Thanks. You too. We'll get 'em next time."

His encouraging words clearly fell flat. She turned away without responding, then hurried across the yard to return the bandannas to Mrs. Jackson. Man, what had he done? Tonight was supposed to be a casual evening meant to help people reconnect. So not a big deal.

Then why did he feel like he'd let Savvy down?

Early Monday morning, Savannah parked her car in front of Levi's house, grabbed her tote bag and her insulated mug filled with coffee, then headed for his front door. She'd agreed to stay with Wren that morning because Levi had to get to a staff meeting at the store before they opened. After attending church yesterday, then going to last night's party and participating in the three-legged race, her stomach danced with nervous energy. She wasn't apprehensive to see him, because nothing had happened between them—except she'd nearly told him everything when he'd mentioned family secrets. Yeah, okay, so he'd been joking, but his words had touched a nerve. Left her so flustered that she'd made them lose the race.

She slowly climbed the three steps to his front door and knocked softly. Coming back to Opportunity hadn't been bad, even though it wasn't what she had planned for her future. This wasn't the time to lose sight of her goal, though. She needed a permanent teaching position.

And her interactions with Levi were starting to cloud her perspective.

Especially after the way he'd looked at her when she helped Wren with her hair. They'd agreed to fake a romantic relationship—emphasis on *fake*. A ploy designed to help her feel more comfortable during their reunion activities and to help him get over Tori. Or at least, *look* as though he was getting over Tori. But his kindness, blended with the tender way he looked after Wren... Well, all that was quite genuine.

Wasn't it? Levi's admirable traits conspired against her walled-off heart. Made her question why she'd agreed to his unconventional scheme.

He opened the door. "Hey."

His smile made her heart do a little loop-the-loop. Why did he get to look that handsome first thing on a Monday?

"Good morning," she said.

Levi raked his fingers through still-damp hair as he stepped back. "Come on in."

The spicy scent of his aftershave lingered in the air. Savvy took a sip of her coffee, hoping to cleanse the palate. She set her oversize canvas tote bag on the floor.

He tilted his head for a closer inspection. "What do you have there?"

"Oh, I brought over a couple of puzzles and a board game. A simple matching one that Wren and I can play together. There's also paper and finger paint, but don't worry, I brought an old shirt she can wear to cover—"

"Whoa. Hang on a minute." Levi rubbed his fingertips along his clean-shaven jaw. "I'd like for her to go to story time at the library. It starts at ten, and then my mom's going to pick her up after that. She'll watch her so that you can get back to work on the float for the parade."

Oh.

He reached past her, lifting his keys off the hook. "Wren's still sleeping, so you might have to wake her up soon so she has plenty of time to get dressed and eat breakfast."

She sipped her coffee to keep from saying something she shouldn't. So much for her grand plans. If his mom was available, why did he need her help today?

Levi turned away, clearly looking for something.

"If you're looking for your phone, it's on the coffee table."

"Thanks." He flashed her a half smile, swooped into the living room, then grabbed his phone and strode toward her. Hesitating, he stopped before grabbing his backpack. His brow furrowed. "What's wrong?"

"Nothing."

"Savvy, you look like I stole your lunch box. What happened? What did I say?"

"I've been thinking about Wren and all that she's been through." Savannah kept her voice low just in case Wren popped out of bed. Or tiptoed down the hall to listen in, unnoticed. "Maybe she should choose how she wants to spend her day. I mean, if you've already got something planned with your mom, I thought she and I could hang out. Take it easy."

Levi twisted his key chain around on his finger. "But I want her to interact with other kids. Story time is free, and it lasts less than an hour."

"She already tried Vacation Bible School. It wasn't her favorite."

He tucked his phone in his pocket, then hooked his backpack strap over one shoulder. "But she needs structure. The social worker said her home life was chaos."

"She's also a young child who's likely endured a lot," Savannah gently reminded him. "A quiet morning here with me is not exactly chaos."

Sighing, he reached for the door. "Look, I'm running late, so if you could please take her to story time, I would really appreciate it. I'll check in later to see how things are going."

"Sounds good. Have a great day."

He stepped outside, gently pulling the door closed behind him.

She turned in a slow circle, surveying the scene. A pile of unfolded laundry had been dumped onto the couch. Unopened mail sat on the kitchen counter, next to a neat stack of dishes.

Half-tempted to tidy up, she set down her coffee. Nope. Chores were not part of their agreement. Besides, he'd kind of aggravated her with his comments. So she picked up her bag and sat down at the counter, carefully slid a stack of mail out of the way and opened her laptop. As soon as she logged on to the internet, she quickly opened the school district's website and clicked on the link for available jobs.

After scrolling through a half dozen options, her

breath hitched when the posting for the art teacher position appeared last. *Finally.* She pumped her fist, then clicked the link and scanned through the requirements, just as Wren came out of her bedroom. She was wearing a faded blue T-shirt and thin striped shorts that had seen better days.

"Hi, Wren." Savannah smiled and closed her laptop. "Did you sleep well?"

"Where's Lee-by?"

"He had to go to work. I'm going to hang out with you this morning. What would you like for breakfast?"

Wren stalked past her, flopped down on the couch and fumbled with the remote.

"How about scrambled eggs? Maybe some cereal? Or do you like to start with toast?"

Still ignoring her, Wren turned on the television and started watching a morning talk show.

"Wren, we're not watching TV right now. Please turn it off and come help me make your breakfast."

"No!" Wren wailed. "No breakfast!"

Oh boy. It was going to be one of *those* days.

Savannah stepped in front of Wren, blocking her view of the television. Wren craned her neck to try to see around her. "Sweet girl, we are not starting our day with television."

"Lee-by lets me."

"Levi's not here." She gently extracted the remote from the little girl's hand, turned off the television and gestured for Wren to come to the kitchen. "Let's get some breakfast, and then we can get ready to go to story time at the library. Doesn't that sound fun?"

"Not fun at all." Wren flung herself face down into the pile of unfolded clothes and burst into tears.

Savannah blew out a long breath. As Wren cried into the clean laundry, Savannah closed her eyes and prayed. *Lord, please give me extra patience today. Help me show Wren that I care about her and I'm here to keep her safe.*

She'd taught a handful of students who had lived in foster homes, but none as young as Wren. Or this spunky. Somehow, she'd find ways to establish a positive bond with Wren. Not just because it was the right thing to do, but also because she feared if word spread that she couldn't handle a four-year-old, she wouldn't get a permanent teaching job.

"Where's Jasper?" Levi stood in the doorway of the break room at the store. A box of doughnuts sat in the middle of the table. Coffee percolated in the machine on the counter beside the sink.

Dad pulled paper plates and napkins from a shopping bag. "He's running late."

Levi bit back a frustrated groan. He'd been running late, too, and he wasn't proud of how his conversation had gone with Savvy, but he'd still made the effort to get here on time. "How late?"

"We're probably going to have to push the meeting back to ten thirty."

"So we're having a meeting while the store is open? How's that going to work?"

"Your mom's going to come by and cover things for us." Dad crossed over to the fridge and pulled out his favorite vanilla creamer.

Irritation simmered in his core, threatening to boil over. "When is she coming by? Because I've already asked her to pick up Wren from the library at eleven fifteen."

"You might have to rearrange your plans, son. Sometimes people oversleep."

"Are you kidding me? I can't ask Savannah to keep Wren longer because Jasper didn't hear his alarm. She's supposed to be working on the parade float for our store, remember?"

Dad crumpled up a receipt and tossed it in the trash can beside the door. "Like I said, sometimes people oversleep. Maybe you should have thought about how taking on single parenthood would affect your career."

Levi scoffed. "Maybe *you* should consider how letting Jasper be a slacker is impacting business."

Dad pinned him with a fiery look. "Excuse me?"

"My brother didn't show up for work on time. His inability to get out of bed is forcing the rest of us to rearrange our plans for the day. It's weird how you're excusing his laziness but criticizing my choices."

The whir of the refrigerator filled the tense silence. A muscle in Dad's jaw twitched. "Did you ever consider that if you and Tori hadn't split up, maybe you wouldn't be a single dad?"

Wow, don't hold back. He drew a withering breath. "This is an emergency foster care placement, Dad. That means Wren literally had nowhere else to go."

"Yeah, that's too bad." Dad stepped around him, opened the cabinet and pulled out a mug with the store's logo on the side. "Want some coffee?"

"No, I want to have the staff meeting like we planned."

Dad filled his mug. A tendril of steam curled up from the coffeepot. "That's pointless since Jasper's not here."

"Unbelievable." Spots peppered his vision. Half a dozen sharp retorts zipped through his head. None worth popping off for, though. He'd already said enough. Levi hung his backpack on an empty hook by the door, then strode out into the store. He flipped the sign around from Closed to Open, unlocked the door, then got the till from the safe in the back and installed it in the register.

The familiar routine of starting a new day brought him a little comfort.

But he was still too angry. After pulling his phone from his back pocket, he crafted a terse five-word text.

Hurry up. You are late.

With irritation still humming through his veins, he hit Send, then jammed his phone back into his jeans pocket. Wasn't like Jasper was going to answer him, anyway.

Dad strode out of the break room and came toward him, a steely glint in his eyes. "Do you want to tell me what that was all about?"

Levi made sure they had plenty of shopping bags on hand and a jar of pens on the counter before he selected a station to play music on the overhead speakers. Performing those tasks gave him a minute to gather his thoughts.

"I was pretty clear, Dad. My brother's not responsible enough to get out of bed and get to work on time, and you chose to criticize *me*. I don't appreciate it."

"Look…" His father sighed, rubbing his palm across the top of his bald head. "You've not been yourself since you and Tori went your separate ways. I just can't figure out why you've added a child to your life."

"And I can't figure out why you don't support my decision." Levi crossed his arms over his chest and fought to keep the anger from his voice. "Kids need stable homes. Yes, ideally, I would be married and there would be two of us, but that's not what Tori wanted. I wasn't going to turn my back on a helpless child who was living in a very dangerous environment."

"But you're in over your head."

"Not sure where you're getting that."

Dad stared at him like he'd sprouted an extra limb. "You're struggling to balance childcare with work, you've had to—"

"Doesn't every working parent have that problem? Most people who foster have other responsibilities too."

Dad threw his hands in the air. "I don't know why I'm even trying to talk some sense into you. My mistake. Clearly you have it *all* figured out."

Ouch. Dad's words provoked a mixture of pain and surprise. He counted to three silently before he responded, half expecting his father to retreat. When Dad gave him that same flinty-eyed stare, Levi pressed on.

"Here's the deal. Savannah is helping with Wren and trying to come up with a float for our store with almost no resources and a limited amount of time. So if you'd like to alleviate some of her stress, then speak to Jasper about his priorities instead of making the rest of us rearrange our lives to accommodate him."

"Whatever Savannah needs for that float, she can have it," Dad said, bracing his elbows on the counter beside the register.

"You don't mean that. You and Jasper both told me there wasn't much in the budget. Besides, the parade's ten days away. Even if we gave her an unlimited budget, how would she get what she needed in time?"

"She's creative. I'm sure she'll come up with something."

Oy. Levi massaged his forehead with his fingertips. Before he could say anything else, the door opened and two customers came in. Dad conveniently disappeared into the break room. Then Levi spent the next forty-five minutes helping the guys pick out the gear they needed to hike in the area. Shortly after ten, Jasper strode in, showered, shaved and toting a drink carrier from the coffee shop.

"Hey." He grinned sheepishly. "Sorry I'm late. Hope coffee will make up for it."

Levi's phone chimed with an incoming text. He pulled out his phone and read the message from Savvy.

Wren has been involved in a biting incident at the library. Please come as soon as you can. We'll be waiting outside.

Levi's stomach plummeted. "Oh no."

Jasper paused from unpacking the coffee cups. "What's wrong?"

"It's Wren. She's at story time at the library, and something happened. I've got to go."

"Levi, wait," Jasper called out after him.

"I can't." Levi jogged into the break room,

grabbed his backpack, then hurried down the hall and pushed through the back exit. His father's criticism echoed in his mind.

You're in over your head.

Yeah, well, maybe Dad was right. There wasn't a reasonable explanation for how much he cared about her. He couldn't define the feeling that had propelled him to take action and bring a child into his home without much support. Clearly his behavior baffled his own family. He just knew he couldn't turn his back on Wren.

"Lee-by is going to be so mad," Wren sobbed, plodding along beside Savannah as they crossed the library parking lot.

"Wren, I don't think he's going to be mad," Savannah said, gently pressing her palm against Wren's shoulder. "He cares about you very much."

"No," Wren insisted. "He's going to be so mad. I'm in big trouble."

Oh, poor thing. There had to be a way to gently guide her out of her fear and teach her that biting wasn't okay. Her fear over Levi's anger mattered too. Savannah couldn't recall ever seeing Levi get angry—well, maybe in a skirmish with Jasper, but he would never hurt Wren. Savannah was 100 percent certain of that.

"Sweet pea, biting is not okay. Can you tell me more about what happened?" She already knew the basics from the library staff, but she thought Wren should give her the full story.

"That girl sat in my place," Wren said, her little brow furrowed.

"Let's go over here. There are some swings. We can sit and talk." Savannah checked both ways before guiding Wren across the street to a small park with a playground. Thankfully, there weren't any kids around, so they could choose their swings. Wren headed for the oversize disc suspended from the overhead frame with three ropes.

She struggled to climb on. "Will you help me, please?"

Savannah hesitated. This wasn't supposed to be a fun outing. She needed to get the full story. Maybe they could chat while Wren enjoyed the freedom of not having to share the novelty swing.

"I'll help you if you'll tell me what happened. Deal?"

Wren gave a solemn nod.

Savannah gave her a boost onto the swing. As soon as Wren was settled, Savannah gently pushed the rubber circle. "Do you come to story time a lot?"

Wren shook her head, then tucked her chin to her chest.

"So how did you know that was your spot?"

"It just is. I have to be close. I need to see *all* the pages."

"I understand." She couldn't fault Wren for

wanting a front-row seat. Definitely an age-appropriate preference, especially when there had been at least a dozen kids clambering for a seat on the librarian's multicolored rug.

Wren clutched the ropes with both hands. "The girl, she didn't move."

"Did you ask her to move?"

"Sort of."

"Did you use kind words, or did you just tell her?"

"Told her."

"And when she didn't move, what happened?"

"I bit her on the arm. Then she moved."

Savannah clamped her lips tight to avoid laughing. There wasn't anything humorous about this. It was hard not to smile at Wren's matter-of-fact truth-telling. Or her confidence in her own flawed way of solving the problem.

"Wren, when Levi gets here, you're going to have to tell him more about what happened."

Wren gasped and her eyes grew wide. "No, you can't tell him."

"Sweetheart, I already have," Savannah said.

Suddenly, Wren scampered off the swing and ran toward the jungle gym.

"Wren, wait." Savannah trotted after her. "You can't run away."

Wren climbed inside a purple cube-shaped tunnel. Just out of reach.

Savannah slowed her steps and sat down on the

nearby stairs. Close enough so that Wren could hear her but far enough away that hopefully she wouldn't feel threatened. "I had to tell Levi. He's the grown-up who's in charge of you right now, so he needs to know what's going on."

"Why can't you be in charge of me?"

"Well, foster care doesn't work like that. Sometimes I help when Levi has to do other things, like work at the store."

"I don't like the store. It's boring there." Wren's voice filtered out through the small holes dotting the tunnel. Through the openings, Savannah could see the little girl poking around with a twig.

"Wren, it's summertime, and the grown-ups have to do our jobs. As often as we can, we will plan fun activities for you, like story time and the parade."

"And eating fun snacks," Wren added. "The snacks at the three-legged race were really good."

"True. The Jacksons have a nice home, and the party food was great." She didn't really want to talk about the race. Candace and her husband had won. Not that she was bitter or anything. "Levi will be here in a few minutes. You'll need to come out of there and speak with him."

"No, I need you to stay with me," Wren whined.

"I need to work on the float for the parade."

"Where's Lee-by's mom?" Wren asked. "I want her to get me. She has the bestest snacks."

Savannah didn't bother to correct the mispronunciation. They had bigger issues to deal with— starting with how Wren evaluated people based on the quality of snacks provided. "I can't make you come out of there, but I wish you would tell me why you're so upset."

"Because I'm in big trouble. Trouble means I'm a bad girl."

"Wren, that is not true. You made a choice, and it wasn't a great choice. Biting is not okay, but that doesn't mean you're a bad kid."

"That's not what my mommy said. Or the mean lady at the big church."

Oh dear. Savannah's heart pinched. She hated that this little girl had endured so much.

But what could she do? How could she ease her heartache and help her understand that she wasn't alone in her struggles?

Adrenaline pulsed through his veins as he pulled into the nearest parking spot in front of the library. He couldn't stand the thought of someone biting Wren. That must've been so traumatic. He turned off the engine and quickly exited the vehicle. Hadn't Savvy's last text said they'd meet him outside? Shielding his eyes from the bright morning sunlight with his hand, he turned in a circle, then checked the benches by the front door and the picnic table under the tree on the lawn. No sign of Wren or Savannah.

Why hadn't he listened? Savannah had tried to

tell him story time wasn't a good idea. And he'd pushed back, so determined that he knew what was best when an actual professional—a teacher who'd spent way more time with kids—had tried to offer her perspective.

Dude, you're an idiot.

He pulled out his phone. A message from Savannah popped up on the screen.

I see you in the library parking lot. We're across the street by the jungle gym.

"Oh, thank You, Lord," he whispered. "Please give me the right words and the courage to be humble."

He pocketed his phone, looked both ways and then jogged across the street. The stricken expression on Savannah's face halted his steps. "What's going on?"

"Wren is inside the purple tunnel, refusing to come out. She's concerned that she's in trouble." Savannah pinned him with a long look. "I have reassured her that you would never punish her and you are not angry."

He winced. Maybe a little angry. Hadn't someone just been bitten? He opened his mouth to object, but Savannah's expression grew fierce. "Because you need to hear the whole story. Right?"

He quickly got the hint that Wren could hear every word. "Right."

Savannah tilted her head toward the small tunnel in a silent prompt for him to take over. He walked over and sank down on the ground beside the purple cube. "Wren, are you okay? I heard you had a rough time at the library."

"Go away."

The words came out barely above a whisper.

"Wren, I—I can't leave you here alone," he said, bracing his elbows on his knees.

"Sabby stays."

"Savvy is still here, but she has other things she needs to do today."

He heard her tossing pebbles against the interior wall. He shot Savannah a helpless look. She stood nearby, her arms across her chest. He didn't deserve any help, not after the way he'd disregarded her insight. But he was really at a loss. She didn't look like she was coming to his rescue anytime soon.

"Come on, Wren. I need you to come out so we can talk about this."

"No."

Oh brother. He stood.

Savannah gave a silent shake of her head. He got the message—he wasn't supposed to back down. Rookie Parenting 101: don't let the preschooler own you. Easier said than done, though. He had no leverage here. Well, maybe some snacks in the car... But luring her out with food didn't feel like the right approach either.

"Wren, I'd like to hear more from you about what happened," he said. "Can you tell me your side of the story?"

More rocks pinged the inside of the tunnel. "I told Sabby already."

He blew out a long breath. She was not going to make this easy.

Savannah motioned for him to follow her.

They walked over to the swings. Far enough away that they could talk quietly but, of course, not out of sight.

"I'm so sorry, Savannah. You tried to tell me she needed some time at the house, and I didn't listen."

"It's all right." She sat down on the swing, grabbed the chain-link handles and gently pushed off with her toe.

He slumped into the swing beside hers and tried to remain still. Swings had never been his thing.

"Come on—swing." Her hair streamed behind her shoulders as she pumped her legs, sailing higher and higher.

"Can I pass? Not exactly my idea of a good time."

She dropped her voice to an exaggerated whisper. "If we look like we're having fun, I'm pretty sure Wren will join us. She likes to swing, and she doesn't want to be ignored."

"Then why is she hiding?"

"Because she bit someone and feels guilty," Savannah said. "She's afraid of what might happen next."

"Does she think I'd...hurt her?" He shuddered at the words. Being an emergency foster parent had tested his patience, and he'd definitely lost sleep over how best to care for Wren. But he'd never in a million years cause harm.

Savannah dragged her sneaker in the dirt to slow the swing. "I don't know what she thinks, but she is afraid that you're angry."

Levi scrubbed his hand over his face. "Driving over here, I thought someone had bitten her. But you're saying she did the biting?"

"Yes," Savannah said. "She bit someone because she didn't like where they were sitting. That's not okay, but we have to be really careful. She already feels ashamed."

He glanced over, studying the concern etched across Savannah's features. "I want to help her and do the right thing. She needs to know that she can't go around biting people until she gets what she wants."

"You are exactly right. In this situation, we have to teach her how to change her behavior in a way that helps her feel secure."

"What does that look like? I'm doing everything I can here, Savvy. She still acts out."

"I know it's not going to be easy," Savannah said. "It won't happen in a couple of weeks. It might not even happen in a couple of months.

The girl she bit is okay, by the way. Wren didn't leave a mark or anything. I asked about her—her mother had already taken her home by the time I got here."

"I'm not sure I can do much about biting in the next few weeks. What if she goes to stay with somebody else? This is only supposed to be a temporary stop."

"You don't know what's going to happen next." Savannah's earnest tone and her compassion for Wren filled his chest with a pleasant warmth. He never would've figured out how to navigate this on his own. "What if you end up being her forever home? Won't you be glad that you made the effort to build a strong foundation?"

Valid point.

"I have no right to ask for your help after I bull-dozed your last suggestion, but...do you have any coping strategies? Because I don't know where to go from here."

"I'm so glad you asked." She leaned closer and lowered her voice. "Wren will probably not be thrilled, so you'll have to stand your ground. I suggest encouraging her to apologize. Since she probably can't write well, encourage her to color a picture. Or help bake some cookies to take to the family of the girl she bit."

Sighing, he tipped his head back. "You're right. On both counts. She needs to apologize, and she won't be excited about it."

Savvy offered an empathetic smile. "You're doing a great job with her, Levi. She's fortunate to have you in her life."

Encouraged by her kind words and sweet smile, Levi pushed to his feet. "Thank you. It hasn't been easy. I need to coax her out of her hiding spot."

"Wait." She discreetly tipped her head toward the jungle gym. "Looks like she's on her way over."

Levi turned and glanced over his shoulder.

Wren was inching her way out of hiding. Slowly, she stood and trudged toward them with her chin dipped low.

"Let her speak first." Savvy's gentle guidance filtered around him. "She might surprise you."

He nodded, willing his features to form a gracious, patient expression.

Wren stopped in front of him, still avoiding eye contact. Her lower lip trembled. "I'm sorry, Lee-by."

Oh, this kid. Everything about her made his heart ache. He sank to the ground until he was eye level. "Wren, I'm not upset with you. Everyone makes mistakes. Would you like a hug?"

Wren drew in a ragged breath, then nodded.

Levi stretched his arms wide, and Wren ran into them.

He hugged her gently, then closed his eyes. *Thank You, Lord.*

They still had miles to go in establishing trust, but this felt like a win. A tiny one, anyway.

Wren pulled back, her eyes shimmering with tears. "Can we go home now?"

Nodding, he stood and swallowed against an unexpected lump lodged in his throat. Dad and Jasper could easily handle the store that afternoon. Wren needed him.

She slipped her hand into his.

He stole a quick glance at Savannah. Sniffling, she wiped at the moisture on her cheeks. When she met his gaze, he offered a grateful smile. "Thank you."

"Of course."

Together, they crossed the street to their cars parked in the library lot. He never would've known how to handle this without Savvy's help. Guilt swept in. He shouldn't have dismissed her insight about story time so quickly. Sure, he'd hired her to babysit and decorate the parade float, but he hadn't anticipated relying on her to coach him through scenarios like this. If Wren stayed with him through the fall, what would he do when Savvy found a teaching job?

Chapter Seven

The ninth inning of the softball game couldn't end soon enough.

Savannah stood in the outfield, dragging the toe of her sneaker through the grass. She fiddled with a loose thread on Wyatt's well-loved mitt and tried to pay attention to whatever was happening at home plate. Her thoughts wandered easily. Since the story-time debacle on Monday, the week had flown by in a blur. She'd kept Wren occupied and put in long hours on the parade float. There was still so much work to do before the parade next week. She'd rather be up to her eyeballs in papier-mâché than spend one more minute playing softball.

Mainly because this particular reunion activity reminded her way too much of her high school PE class. How ironic that she stood here on the field as an adult with almost the exact same cast of characters. The only highlight of the afternoon? Well, two highlights actually—it wasn't raining, and she had a great view of Levi's muscular shoulders.

He'd been roped into playing shortstop, and for all his protests that he didn't want to be part of this particular reunion activity, he'd played well. One of his at-bats had brought in a teammate who'd scored a run, and he'd caught the ball once, making an out for the opposing team. She, on the other hand, had cost her team dearly when the ball dropped onto the grass and rolled between her legs, allowing a runner to get to second base. Then she'd struck out twice. Three cringey details Candace had broadcast to anyone and everyone. Savannah glared at Candace, who was waiting on deck to bat. Why did the woman care so much about winning a casual softball game? And why did Savannah let Candace get to her so easily? Levi glanced over his shoulder and smiled, pulling her from her spiral of negativity. Wow, he was handsome. And such a good sport. Still smiling in spite of his brother and Candace's juvenile behavior.

"Yay, Lee-by!" Wren's adorable cheer drew chuckles from the handful of spectators sitting on the metal bleachers outside the fence.

"You've got this, Candace," Jasper called from the dugout. Their teammate had just struck out. Candace strode toward the batter's box, already yammering at the man who'd volunteered to be the umpire. Jasper and Candace had conveniently been placed on the same team, and they'd made it very clear they fully intended to win. Savannah had never cared about the score in any game in her life. At least, not any sporting event in recent memory. But today she sort of cared. Mostly because she wanted Levi to smile at her again.

"What are you, twelve?" she scolded herself quietly.

The pitcher tossed his first pitch to Candace. *Please not to me, please not to me,* Savannah silently pleaded. Thankfully, Candace swung and missed. Savannah resisted the urge to pump her fist. That wouldn't go over well.

Levi glanced over his shoulder again. "Get ready. This ball might be coming your way."

"No, no, no." Savannah shook her head. "That would not be good. Wanna trade places?"

Levi chuckled. "Nope. Too late. Just keep your eye on the ball and catch it."

Right. Like it was that easy. But she punched her glove with her fist like she'd seen some of the others do.

Levi grinned. "That's my girl."

Her breath hitched. The words on his lips sounded so convincing. Had he said that because he meant it? Or so others would buy into their fake-dating scheme? Tori had been sitting in the bleachers for most of the game, although Savannah didn't risk looking for her now. Just in case the ball did come her way.

Candace's second swing propelled the ball across the baseline toward her own team's dugout.

Foul ball. Candace turned and said something to the umpire. He shook his head. The pitcher caught the ball, then wound up and lobbed the next pitch toward home plate. Candace swung again with a dramatic grunt. This time, her bat connected with the ball and sent it sailing into the air. Anticipation swirled in Savannah's stomach as she squinted into the sun. She never wanted to be the heroine of a softball game, but her fear of the ball coming to her suddenly morphed into something decidedly different. Something that felt a little like determination.

"Oh dear," Savannah said, squinting as she lost sight of the ball in the sun.

"This is you, Savvy," Levi called out.

"I know—that's the problem."

The ball filled her vision again, hurtling toward her. *Don't mess this up.* Somehow, she shuffled her feet to get under it. She squeezed her eyes shut just as the ball landed with a satisfying *thunk* in her mitt. The stinging sensation in her palm was so worth it. A cheer erupted, and Savannah stood perfectly still, afraid to look. But then she opened her eyes, glanced down at her mitt and then blinked in disbelief. *Really?*

Levi jogged toward her, his face split wide with a proud grin.

"I got it." The words left her lips with a gusty breath. She thrust the softball in the air. "I actually caught the ball."

"Way to go." Levi flung his glove to the ground and scooped her into his arms. She held on to the ball with one hand while her brother's mitt slipped away. Levi spun her around in a dizzying circle. Oh, he smelled good. Like the outdoors, sunshine and spicy aftershave. Her heart pounded in anticipation as he nudged back the brim of his cap. Then he set her on her feet, and his eyes dipped toward her lips. She swallowed hard, the sound of their teammates celebrating fading away as he slowly leaned in for a kiss. His lips were soft against hers, but doubts crept into her mind. Was this really what he wanted? Was this just a ploy to further their fake relationship? She pushed back these thoughts, allowing herself to enjoy the warmth that spread through her body when his palm rested at the base of her neck.

His touch was gentle yet reverent, which made her pulse quicken even more. He pulled her closer and deepened the kiss. But then a callous comment about their public display of affection snapped her out of the moment. Wren must have seen them kiss. Had Tori? Panic flooded every inch of her body, and she reluctantly pulled away from Levi.

"What have we done?"

Wow. Okay. He stepped back and tugged his baseball cap back into place. "I'm sorry. Maybe we shouldn't—"

"Kiss her again!"

The teasing phrase bellowed from somewhere in the dugout deepened the pink splotches on Savvy's cheeks.

He hadn't meant to kiss her in front of everyone like that, but when he'd seen how excited she was from catching that fly ball—her eyes wide with awe—he had to demonstrate his admiration.

Her gaze darted past him. "I guess that means we won."

He shifted his weight and spotted Tori, sitting in the third row in the metal bleachers alone. His heart sank at the sight of her getting up and leaving. He couldn't read her features from here, but the swiftness of her departure suggested she wasn't thrilled. Levi curled his fingers into a fist. It was childish, yes, but it still hurt to have been rejected by her. They'd had plans—plans that involved a future in Opportunity together—before she'd applied to dental school without telling him. This fake relationship with Savannah seemed like a great way to make Tori jealous and regret her decision, though he didn't want to hurt Savannah in the process.

Because that kiss had definitely changed things between them.

He retrieved her discarded mitt and passed it back to her. "You should be proud of yourself," he said, admiring the ball she clutched in her hand. "What an incredible catch."

She tucked the ball inside her mitt. "That was

totally random. I usually try to avoid flying objects."

The sparkle in her eyes made him want to hear more of her quick wit, so they strolled together toward the infield.

"Don't stress over that kiss, okay? It was all for show, right?" she blurted out unexpectedly.

His heart sank. No, it wasn't just for show. "Yeah, of course—just wanted to make everyone think we were together."

"Well, by the way people are looking at us and cheering, I'd say our plan worked," she said with a bounce in her step. "Are you and Wren going to stay for lunch? My parents are helping serve food."

"If Wren doesn't get tired soon, then we'll stick around," he said. "How about you?"

The families of their classmates had already set up coolers behind the dugouts and tables covered with plastic tablecloths for desserts and bags of chips.

Savannah skirted around Candace and Jasper, who were talking with some other members of their team on the first baseline. "Yeah, I might stick around for a little bit too."

The smell of sizzling hot dogs and burgers made his stomach grumble. He followed Savannah, hoping to pass through the gate in the chain-link fence near the dugout and find Wren. Then their former classmate David stepped in front of them.

"Nice work there." He extended his palm outward, and Savannah slapped it. "Great catch."

"Thanks." A smile played on her lips as she continued on her way.

Levi lingered near the entrance to take a final glance at his twin. Jasper lifted his chin in acknowledgment of the game's result, though he certainly didn't look pleased with the outcome.

Levi grinned. Man, Jasper really didn't like to lose.

"Lee-by!" Wren darted toward the field, her skirt caked with dirt and her face sporting a ketchup splotch. "Did you guys kiss?"

Savannah gasped at the question. Warmth heated his neck. He hadn't stopped to think about what his public display of affection for Savannah—whether fake or not—might do to Wren.

"Hey, kiddo." Levi swept Wren's hair back from her forehead. "We did kiss. And how about Savvy catching that fly ball? Pretty amazing, right?"

Okay, so maybe that was a lame attempt at redirection.

Wren's smooth brow furrowed. "I don't like baseball. Can you find me a juice box? Please?"

Levi placed his hand on her shoulder and steered her toward the coolers. "Sure thing. The drinks are this way."

He didn't regret kissing Savannah. At all. But Wren's response was hard to interpret. As he helped her find something to drink, he couldn't shake the uneasy feeling that his impulsive action might've upset their fragile bond.

Don't make it weird. We just kissed. No big deal.

Savannah sat in her canvas camping chair, a plate with a hot dog, potato salad and watermelon on her lap, still trying to process the thrill of that kiss. The warmth of Levi's touch was undeniable, as well as the affection in his eyes. Was she imagining things? He dragged another chair up next to her and sat down, setting his plate on his lap. He shot her a grin, and she felt a blush creep into her cheeks as she tried to focus on her food.

"People are still talking about you over by the dessert table," he said, popping open his can of soda with a loud crack.

Oh no. She swallowed a bite of food quickly, then reached for her water bottle. "That is not something I want to hear."

"Why not?" His smile widened, and her stomach did backflips. "That was an awesome catch. You helped our team win the game."

Cheers erupted from the nearby bleachers as the next team scored a run.

"Ah, I get it." The knowing expression on Levi's face made her pulse race again. "You think they're talking about that kiss."

Her heart started to flutter even more. "I mean, yeah. If it were me, I would be talking about that kiss."

Oh, wow. She hadn't meant to say that out loud.

Levi chuckled softly, sending another wave of heat rushing through her body. He leaned closer. "So, on a scale from one to ten, how would you rate that kiss compared to catching that fly ball?"

She lifted her hand and used it to shield her face, as if hiding her expression might encourage him not to ask any more questions. "Oh brother. Your humility is remarkable."

"You haven't answered me." His voice was low and deep. A playful reminder that he was still waiting for a response.

"Because it's not a fair question." She picked up her slice of watermelon and took a bite, chewing slowly and deliberately in an effort to buy time.

"No comparison, then—is that what you're saying?"

As she fumbled for her napkin and wiped the juice trickling down her chin, she could feel his gaze burning into her skin. He was waiting for an answer. And honestly, so was she.

"You really want me to rate our kiss?" Her words were barely louder than a whisper, but she knew he had heard them.

The corners of his mouth curved into a smile. "Sure do."

She set aside her unfinished watermelon and tucked the napkin beneath her plate. Drawing in a fortifying breath, she met Levi's gaze again.

"Still waiting here," he reminded her with a teasing glint in his eye.

Her lips twitched in response. "Fine. Your kiss was excellent—top-tier stuff."

He flashed an amused grin. "Shall I give myself ten out of ten stars?"

"Without a doubt." She paused. "But it can't happen again."

The smile left his face. "Why not?"

"Because I know you kissed me only to convince people that we're together."

He studied her long and hard before turning his attention back to his cheeseburger. The air around them had become thick with unspoken tension. She forced herself to keep her eyes locked on his. "It was fake, right?"

He hesitated. "Of course. All part of the plan."

She was supposed to feel relieved by this news…wasn't she? That was the second time she'd asked him, and his answer hadn't changed. Instead, she felt a tightness in her chest that could only be disappointment.

"When you took Wren to get her juice, did she ask you any more questions about our kiss?"

He shook his head. "I didn't offer any additional details either."

Savannah picked up her watermelon. "Do you think she's upset?"

"Hard to tell." He took another bite of his cheeseburger.

Had they confused her? When she'd agreed to babysit, decorate the parade float and pretend to be Levi's date to the reunion activities, she hadn't spent much time thinking about how their interactions might impact Wren. But that kiss had been a bit reckless. And the last thing the sweet girl needed was more uncertainty in her life.

"Lee-by, look at me."

He shifted in his seat and glanced toward Wren as she darted around a muddy puddle. "Wren, don't—"

Savannah placed her hand on his arm. "Let her be," she said softly.

He pointed to the forgotten lunch still packaged and sitting next to him. "But she hasn't eaten yet."

"She ate something, because there's still ketchup on her cheek. If she's hungry, she'll let you know. Don't worry," Savannah reassured him.

With a mischievous giggle, Wren jumped right into the middle of the puddle.

Levi covered his eyes with his hand. "And those shoes I just bought her..."

"It's okay. The mud will all wash out. Besides, listen to that laugh—she's so happy."

He reached for his soda. Their eyes met as laughter filled the area around them. Oh, she wished desperately that she could kiss him again. But she resisted. Pulling her gaze away, she continued eating her lunch while enjoying the sunshine and incredible smell of grass and dirt as they watched Wren together. She wanted nothing more than for this to be the start of something real between them, but deep down, she knew better. She was merely a filler until he recovered from his breakup with Tori. It would take many months before he'd fully heal, and even longer for Savannah to forget about their amazing first kiss. Though she had told Levi it was great, any chance of another one was gone.

Leave it to Candace to plan a white water rafting trip two days before the parade. Didn't she have any last-minute painting to finish? Or balloons to inflate? Because Savannah had some of both to tackle. Frowning, she stood in line behind Levi, waiting outside the school bus that had been converted into a makeshift closet. They had to put on all the appropriate gear they needed before claiming their places in the inflatable rafts. A light rain fell from a gray sky, and the ball cap she'd pulled on before she'd left the house offered little protection.

Levi cast a concerned glance over his shoulder. "I can drive you home. You look miserable."

"I'm not miserable. Just stressed about getting the float finished in time," Savannah said. "Besides, I haven't been rafting since I was a kid, so I didn't want to skip this."

Or miss out on a chance to spend time with Levi. She'd rehashed nearly every detail of the kiss with her sisters last night because they hadn't been at the game. Juliet and Hayley had pressed her for more information. To the point of being annoying, really. Savannah had omitted the part about Levi persuading her to rate the kiss; her sisters would never get over that. What she wouldn't give to be wrapped in his warm embrace right this minute. Shivering, she pushed her hands into the front pocket of her hoodie.

A few minutes later, after she'd passed through the school bus and put on her rubber boots, rain gear, life jacket and helmet, she picked her way along the rocky riverbank. Levi followed her to the place where the rafts had been beached.

"Hey," Levi said, his kind eyes skimming her face. "Are you sure you're all right?"

She eyed the churning gray water as it rushed past a boulder lodged in the river bottom. "Would now be a bad time to mention we have almost five hundred balloons to inflate? I should've said something before now. I'd planned to get my sisters to help me, but we stayed up late last night talking. Then I applied for that teaching job," she said, squeezing the words from her tight throat. She stopped short of mentioning how listing her references had made her want to delete the entire application.

His forehead crinkled. "I didn't realize you had so much on your mind. No one is going to judge you if you'd rather stay on shore. This is supposed to be fun."

Behind him, she spotted Tori and her date exiting the bus with their gear. The guy said something, and Tori tipped back her head, laughing.

"I'm in." Savvy forced a smile. "We had a deal. I promised you I'd be here. We can inflate balloons later. The parade's two whole days away."

Levi didn't look convinced. He reached down and buckled the top buckle on her life jacket. "There."

His attention to her safety made warmth bloom in her chest. *What a thoughtful guy.*

Levi put his helmet on, then angled his head toward the raft. "Let's grab spots in this one. I know the guide, Keith. He's got a ton of experience."

"Experienced is good. I'm not the best swimmer in the world." Savannah followed him, moving slowly in her clunky rubber boots. Jasper, Candace, David and his girlfriend, Alexis, joined them.

Ugh. She'd really hoped that Candace would ride in a different raft. Where was her husband? And Jasper's new fiancée?

A muscle in Levi's jaw jumped. So, she wasn't the only one who was irritated by their decision to pick Keith's raft.

C'mon, don't be a Negative Nellie. This is supposed to be fun.

Savannah pushed past her frustration over Candace and Jasper's proximity and focused her attention on Keith as he demonstrated how to hold the paddles properly. But she couldn't shake the ominous feeling that hovered over her. Why was this so stressful? Sure, it had been more than a decade since she'd floated down the river, but that didn't mean today couldn't be enjoyable.

Still, she shot one last longing glance toward the vehicles in the parking lot nearby.

Levi gently nudged her shoulder with his own. "Last chance to bail."

"I'm fine," she whispered. The weight of Jasper's gaze warmed her skin. She forced her eyes to meet his, determined not to let him see that she was anxious. Ever since their encounter at his engagement party, she'd been walking on eggshells, certain that somehow Jasper was going to unearth her secret. The real reason why she had to leave Colorado. Not that she could blame him for wanting to protect his twin brother. But she wasn't a threat. All she wanted was a second chance. A fresh start. Was that really too much to ask?

"The Poplar River is considered Class 3 Rapids. So it's a great place to start if you haven't been in a raft before," Keith said, grinning as he glanced around their circle of six. "I know some of you grew up here and probably spent some quality time near the river. For the sake of everyone involved, let's go over our safety protocols. First, we need to talk about what to do if you have an out-of-boat experience."

Savvy's breath hitched. "An out-of-boat what?"

"It's rare," Levi said. "Especially on this river."

"We don't anticipate anybody leaving the boat," Keith continued. "We have to be prepared, though."

"Can you flip us on purpose?" Candace asked, bouncing up on her toes. Her eyes sparkled with anticipation.

Keith grimaced. "I'm afraid not. I actually get a bonus at the end of the season if I keep all my passengers in the raft."

Candace heaved a dramatic sigh. "Where's the fun in that?"

"Remember your tripod," Keith continued. "Your bottom in your seat, both feet in proper position inside the boat and your paddle. Those three points of contact will keep you safe, and if you follow my instructions, you'll have a fun, safe ride. Any questions?"

"Take us to the rapids," Candace said, pumping a fist in the air. "Come on, it'll be great. David's girlfriend has never done this before. Right, Alexis?"

"Nothing like this in Oklahoma." Alexis grinned. "Bring on the rapids. Can't wait!"

Savannah stifled a groan. Of course Alexis had to be the fearless type. *Super.*

Making sure her feet were wedged in the proper

spaces anchored to the floor of the raft, exactly as Keith had instructed her, Savannah swallowed hard against the sour taste stinging the back of her throat. *What in the world?* She'd never been this anxious near fast-moving water. Maybe her ongoing conflicts were adding to her anxiety.

"Ready?" Levi took his position beside her in the raft.

She managed a quick nod, then tightened her grip on her paddle.

Keith pushed them away from the bank, then hopped into his spot at the back. Raindrops spattered her cheeks. A cool breeze rippled across the valley, making the tree branches dip and sway. They picked up speed as Keith guided them farther down the river. David, Alexis, Candace and Jasper kept up a steady stream of conversation. Savvy tried to pay attention, but she couldn't pry her gaze away from the water swirling around their raft.

Hundreds, maybe even thousands, of people had floated down the Poplar without incident. Visitors to Opportunity rated it as one of their favorite activities. So maybe she just needed to relax. Savor the beauty of God's creation. Exhaustion and stress had filled her head with worst-case scenarios. Why did she have to be such a worrier?

"Everybody hang on." Keith's instruction jolted her back to reality. The churlish water sprayed up over the bow of the raft as they dipped down into the trough of the current. Frothy white water shot up over the side of the inflatable craft. She gasped as the frigid droplets sprayed over her, sending an icy-cold rivulet down inside her rain gear.

Candace's obnoxious laughter punctuated the air. Savannah gritted her teeth.

Hold on. You can do this. It will all be over soon.

She repeated the silent advice as she dropped her oar and clawed at the handholds attached to the raft.

"How are you doing?" Levi called out, his gaze finding hers.

But she didn't have time to respond because the raft suddenly spun around. Now she rode backward, unable to see the river ahead.

"Oh, please, no." She twisted in her seat and glanced over her shoulder. Disoriented, her vision tunneled. Panic welled. The raft struck an obstacle in the river. Hard. The pain rocketed through her spine. She cried out. The last thing she saw before she went over the side was the horror on Levi's face.

He had to help her. Levi's heart raced as he searched the landscape, looking for a way to rescue Savannah from the river. Alexis and David had both been thrown overboard as well, leaving himself, Candace, Jasper and Keith.

"Savvy isn't a strong swimmer," Levi shouted. "Hurry up, Keith. Take charge!"

"I am. Don't you dare try to jump in after her. Got it?" Keith gave him a stern look.

Levi clenched his jaw and looked away. The raft tilted and he hung on, afraid they'd capsize. The water was icy cold, and Savannah had already been shivering on the riverbank before they'd set off. Angry gray clouds had rolled in. Rain spattered his face. He swiped at the moisture with his hand, then narrowed his gaze, desperate not to lose sight of her. Up ahead, the river took a sharp turn. A whirlpool churned in its center, making Levi's stomach sink. A waterfall dropped into the river from a fissure in the mountainside, producing a heavy mist that hung like fog around them while Keith steered the raft closer to Savannah. Why weren't they going faster? She was getting farther away from them with every passing second.

David had managed to grab a tree limb hanging over the edge of the riverbank. He'd looped his arm around Alexis's torso and held her against him. Levi's chest squeezed. Alexis had a gash in her forehead. David clung to the spindly branches, fear etched in his features.

"Savannah's lost her paddle," Levi called over his shoulder to Keith. "We need to throw her a rope."

"There's calmer waters up around the bend.

She'll be fine," Keith insisted, his expression tense as he maneuvered the raft through the angry water. "Look, she's floating—and she's got her feet pointed up. Just like I taught her."

Levi wrapped his fingers around his paddle's handle. They had to push through these rapids to get back to shore. The other raft carrying Tori, her date and four other people was nowhere in sight. Levi looked back at Keith and Jasper. The trees behind them were thinning out. Keith frowned, clutching his paddle tighter as he guided the raft downstream. Levi prayed for guidance, for direction, but he knew it was up to him.

He squared his shoulders and focused on gripping his side of the raft while keeping an eye on the water ahead of them. Savannah was gulping for air, but she wasn't flailing around and, thankfully, hadn't lost consciousness. They had to find a way to safety without capsizing or losing anyone else.

"We need to throw the rope to David and Alexis." Jasper reached for the bag holding the coiled rope. "They're closer."

"No, we don't." Levi snatched the bag from the floor of the raft. "David's holding on to the branch."

Jasper's mouth formed a grim line. He balled his fists in his lap.

"Hey," Keith said. "Settle down, you two. I need you to let me be the guide here. Got it, Levi?"

Jasper leaned in close. "Keith's right. You've got to let him lead."

Candace whipped out her phone. "While you guys sit here and argue, I'm calling 911."

"We're not arguing!" all three men bellowed.

She rolled her eyes, then stabbed at her phone's buttons and pressed the device to her ear. Her body swayed with the movements of the raft bouncing along downriver. "Hello? Yes, this is Candace Finch. We have three people fallen overboard on the Poplar River—one of them is bleeding pretty badly. We need help here fast."

"Tell them to meet us at the lookout spot. They'll know what I mean," Keith directed.

Candace nodded and repeated Keith's instructions to the person on the other line. "Keith says you should meet us at the lookout and that you'll know what he means."

"Real creative emergency-action plan," Levi sneered. His patience had been worn thin.

He laid his oar aside, took hold of a bag, untwisted the rope from it and chucked it with all his might in Savannah's direction.

"Catch hold of that rope, Savvy!"

Please grab it.

She was struggling in the wild waters. Her life jacket was keeping her afloat, but her lips were turning blue. Savannah swam desperately in an attempt to reach the rope, but it was no use. She was too far away from its reach.

Keith frowned and shook his head. "You did not just do that. We can only throw our ropes within seventy-five feet of another person."

Oops. "She's farther downstream now," Levi said, gripping his helmet with both hands. "I had to do something."

"EMS is on the way," Candace said, stowing her phone out of sight. "That's good news, right?"

Levi shook his head. "We have to get Savvy out of that whirlpool."

"That's why I'm telling you to listen," Keith said, his voice tense. "We still have some options."

A heavy feeling settled in Levi's chest. They had to get Savannah back in the raft, and they needed help with David and Alexis too. The rain fell harder, stinging his skin as it was whipped by the wind. Through the gloom, Levi could still make out Savannah, in her yellow rain gear and bright red life jacket, out in the river.

Jasper managed to tug on the rope and toss it to her again. She caught hold of the knotted end this time, and Jasper and Levi worked together to pull her toward them.

Then horror swept across her face, and the rope slipped from her hands.

"My leg! I'm caught!" she cried out.

"What do we do?" Jasper yelled over the roar of the rushing water.

"Just hang on," Keith said firmly. "Stay calm.

We can do this." He nodded at Candace and Jasper, motioning for them to start paddling the boat closer to Savannah. Levi didn't add that he could paddle too. He'd already made enough mistakes today. Slowly but surely, Keith guided the raft until they were close enough for him to reach out with his paddle.

"Let us reel you in," Keith implored.

Savannah nodded, her teeth chattering, as she reached out and clung desperately to the paddle.

"Thank You, Lord," she croaked as Levi, Jasper and Keith gripped her under each arm and hoisted her out of the water. She collapsed on the floor of the raft before breaking into sobs. Levi sat back down, his shoulders sagging with relief. A clump of Savannah's strawberry blond hair was plastered to her cheekbone, and water dripped from the tips of her eyelashes like tears. Her chest heaved as she gasped for breath.

"We're glad you made it back in the boat," Jasper mumbled, giving her arm an awkward pat.

Savannah gave a tiny nod as if acknowledging their concern before brushing at the water on her face with trembling fingers. Levi wanted to reassure her that everything was okay, but instead he sat quietly, trying not to vomit. His stomach roiled with guilt, and he wished it would stop so he could think straight.

They'd almost lost her. He opened his mouth

to speak. The words didn't come. His whole body shook. What if his stupidity had cost Savannah her life?

"Ugh, how embarrassing. Who falls overboard on a basic river-rafting trip?" Savannah huddled under the blanket Hayley had brought her.

"Stop beating yourself up over it. Accidents happen," Juliet said sympathetically, setting down a mug of steaming tea on the table in front of her. "And here's some sugar, too, for your tea."

"Oh, wow, thank you so much." Savannah offered her sisters grateful glances. "I'm sorry I'm being such a baby."

"You have my permission to complain." Hayley plopped down next to Savannah on the couch. "That must have been scary."

Savannah shook her head and shifted away from the blanket, leaning forward to grab her tea. "I don't think I want to do it again," she said. "Have you heard how everyone else is doing? Someone mentioned that Alexis might have a concussion."

Juliet grabbed her phone and checked it. "Nothing new," she said, shaking her head. Her friend was one of the paramedics who'd been at the scene, but there was no new information.

"Movie?" Hayley suggested, grabbing for the remote. But before they could decide on what to watch, there was a knock at the door.

"I'll get it," Juliet offered, heading toward the entryway. Their parents weren't home—they were visiting friends in Fairbanks and weren't due back until tomorrow. Hayley had kept them up to date on Savannah's condition, who only needed an evaluation from the paramedics before being sent home with instructions to stay warm and dry and return to the emergency room if she went into shock.

Juliet came back into the room with Levi and Wren in tow.

Savannah's heart skipped a beat when she saw Wren holding a teddy bear. Wren launched herself across the couch and snuggled up to Savannah, then held the brown-and-tan plushie tight.

"I got this for you, Sabby," she said in a cheerful tone.

"Thank you so much, Wren." Savannah's gaze met Levi's. "You didn't have to do that."

"It was all Wren's idea," he said with a grin. "We were just at the store, getting some soup, when she spotted it in the aisle while I was at the register."

"What's the bear's name?"

Wren shrugged, hugging the bear tighter. "Don't know. You name it."

"I'll have to think about that."

"You could name it Poplar, after the river," Juliet teased.

Savannah recoiled at the suggestion. "Hard pass."

"I think you should name him Wendell," Wren said, planting a dramatic kiss on top of the teddy bear's head.

"Wendell it is." Savannah gave the stuffed animal's arm a gentle shake. "It's nice to meet you, Wendell."

Wren giggled. "Bears don't talk, silly."

"Can I take that for you?" Hayley gestured to the bag in Levi's hands.

"It's only some soup and crackers," he said, glancing at the contents. "And maybe a little ice cream."

Wren's eyes widened in excitement. "Can we have some?"

Savannah looked back at Levi. "That's up to Levi."

"Pleeeease." Wren thrust Wendell into Savannah's lap. "I'll be good. I promise."

A hint of sadness passed over his face as he spoke. "Wren, you don't need to be good just to get some ice cream. That's food, and it's delicious. If these ladies are willing to put some in a bowl for you, then you can have it."

"Come on, Wren." Juliet tipped her head toward the kitchen. "I'm Juliet, by the way. One of Savannah's sisters. Let's go into the kitchen. You can help me scoop the ice cream."

"Yay!" Wren scrambled off the couch, took Juliet's outstretched hand and skipped along beside her.

Hayley's phone rang. She looked at the screen, and her eyes lit up. "Oh. I better take this. Hello?" She left the room.

Savannah sent a grateful smile Levi's way. "Thank you again for everything you did to help me today. I'm not sure I would have gotten out of that river without your help."

"I don't know about that," Levi scoffed, running his fingers through his hair. "Keith knew what he was doing, but it was taking too long for my liking. I shouldn't have tried to intervene."

Savannah noticed the exhaustion in his eyes and gestured at the empty sofa cushions beside her. "Would you like to sit down?"

"Sure," Levi answered sheepishly, looking embarrassed by his intrusion into her home. "I'm sorry. I didn't mean to impose. You must be exhausted."

She waved him off. "My sisters are taking good care of me. Have you heard how David and Alexis are doing?"

Levi sank down on the opposite end of the sofa. "Alexis needs to stay overnight in the hospital for observation. She has a concussion. As far as I know, David's doing fine. Just rattled. Candace's husband picked her up from the rafting office. She wasn't injured."

"And Jasper. Is he okay?"

Levi's jaw tightened. "He's good. Off with Miranda someplace."

"If you don't mind me asking, is there something wrong between the two of you?"

His gaze met hers. "What do you mean?"

"Things seem really tense."

"Yeah, we're still not agreeing on much these days."

She scrunched her nose. "I'm sorry to hear that."

Wren came in from the kitchen, carefully clutching a bowl of ice cream in both hands, the tip of her tongue tucked in the corner of her mouth.

"Do you need a hand there?" Levi asked, scooting over on the couch.

"I have to sit next to Wendell the Bear," Wren insisted, pushing the bowl of ice cream in Levi's direction. "Could you hold this for me?"

"Sure thing." The corner of his mouth crept up in an amused smirk. He seemed just as entertained by her shenanigans as Savannah was. Wren climbed onto the couch and rearranged herself with a theatrical huff.

"All good?"

She nodded, then held her hands out expectantly.

"Should we give some of your ice cream to Wendell?" Levi asked.

"No. His mouth don't work."

Savannah chuckled. "You're right—that is a great point. Would bears like ice cream?"

Wren shrugged, then dug in with her spoon, scooping up a giant bite.

"Whoa, whoa, whoa." Levi held up his palm like a stop sign. "Small bites, there, sweet pea. Or else you'll get an ice-cream headache."

"A what?"

"If you eat cold stuff too quickly, your brain starts to hurt," Savannah said.

Wren looked at her and Levi, clearly uncertain.

"It's true," Levi said. "We wouldn't lie to you."

Wren took a tentative bite of all the ice cream loaded on her spoon.

Juliet joined them, carrying a bowl. "Did you all want some?"

"No, thanks," Levi said.

"I'm good," Savannah added. She leaned forward and carefully picked up her mug of tea. "Warm beverages and blankets are more my style tonight."

It was nice to be here with Wren, acting like Levi belonged. But it felt like a lie. She wasn't sure if her stay in Opportunity would last. They were pretending, just to make everyone else believe they were a couple. Levi had only stopped by to make sure she was okay. They had no romantic feelings between them. This was all an act. One she was becoming increasingly uncomfortable with.

Chapter Eight

He never wanted to tie another knot in a latex balloon again. His fingers ached from the strain, and his eyes burned with fatigue, yet despite drinking multiple cups of coffee and eating a cream-filled doughnut, he still felt exhausted. The only bright spot in this early-morning adventure? Savvy and her sisters' constant chatter as they worked, providing him with a sense of companionship, even if it was just for a few hours.

"Well done," Savvy announced, her hands on her hips as she surveyed the balloon arch they had constructed.

"This was way harder than I thought," Hayley said, sipping her mocha. The vibrant blue-green-and-white creation spanned from one side of the trailer to the other.

At the last minute, Wyatt had convinced a buddy who owned a clothing shop in Fairbanks to loan them a family of three mannequins. Miranda and Jasper had styled them all in hiking clothes from the store. Hayley and Juliet had posed them under the balloons, standing in a papier-mâché meadow and facing a Denali replica. Savvy had filled in empty spaces on the float with artificial boulders, flowers, and a stuffed but lifelike husky dog.

Levi shuddered to think which member of the community had contributed such a huge stuffed animal. Hopefully, Wren wouldn't notice, or she'd be begging for one of her own.

"This is incredible," Juliet said, linking her arms through her sisters'. "I'm so proud of you, Savvy."

At five in the morning, he'd met the girls here at his grandparents' property to finish their float for the parade later that day. He'd campaigned for tying knots and inflating all the balloons the night before, but Savannah feared they'd deflate or, worse, pop. Finally, she admitted her fear that someone might vandalize their masterpiece—a legitimate concern, considering Candace's behavior toward her in the past. He couldn't blame her for being scared, knowing how mischievous people could act on the night before the big parade.

He scrubbed his hand across his face. "Anything else I can do? We need to leave soon."

Wren had stayed the night with his parents. His folks had plenty of responsibilities that morning. They'd probably spend at least an hour setting up tables and chairs at the booths for the festival that took place after the parade. Dad had agreed to bring Wren to meet Levi at the place where the floats lined up. But he'd made it clear he wouldn't be babysitting today.

Savannah stood beside him, tapping one finger against her chin, clearly lost in thought. She'd poured herself into this project, and he could see the pride on her face. Savannah's cheeks were flushed, her eyes bright, her shoulders back and chin up. And her smile. Man, that smile made him want to take her in his arms and kiss her senseless.

"Savvy?" Hayley prompted her. "What else do we need to do?"

"I think we've got it under control, but you can always double-check the candy supply." Savannah pointed to a large storage bin on the barn floor loaded with candy and small plastic buckets.

"Okay, we're on it." Juliet stifled a yawn. "I'll need that caffeine to kick in any minute now."

He followed Hayley's lead and opened up one of the large bags filled with wrapped sugary treats. He poured some candy into the buckets, then passed the bag to Juliet. They checked all the buckets to make sure that they were sufficiently stocked. When they were content that everything was in order, he glanced at his watch—it was already five minutes until nine.

"We should go," he said. "The kids will be lining up soon. We don't want to keep them waiting."

Savannah stood back and snapped a few pictures with her phone.

They'd rounded up a few local kids—elementary school students, plus a couple of responsible middle schoolers to keep them company while they rode through town. All the kids were supposed to meet them at the line-up spot at nine thirty. Given he'd have to drive at a snail's pace to get to town without damaging anything on the float, they needed to leave.

He drained the last of his coffee, then tossed the cup into the trash. "I'll open the doors when you're ready, and we can hitch up the truck to the float."

"Almost ready," she said. "I need two more pictures of my faux mountain, then I'll be set."

He didn't blame her for documenting her work. Once the kids were on board, the float would look like a moving advertisement for outdoor recreation in Denali's foothills, complete with the balloon archway and an incredible replica of the world-famous mountain. This is exactly what he'd wanted, but at the same time, Savvy had done more than he expected. He was eager for Jasper and his dad to see the masterpiece. He still felt the warmth of her arm brushing against his as she'd put together the foundation for the balloons. A fuzzy feeling he couldn't identify continued to swell in his chest.

Love? No, not that soon after Tori. His feelings for Savvy were growing deeper than just respect or admiration. It was something warmer, something brighter. But this wasn't love.

* * *

Savannah took one final lap around the float, making sure everything was in order.

"Hey, Savvy, we really need to go," Levi said from the driver's seat of his grandpa's red pickup. His arm rested on the open window, and he smiled at her.

"I know." She wiped her damp palms across her jean shorts. "I just want it to be perfect."

He chuckled. "It looks great already. Come on, hop in."

She tried not to blush or think about how handsome he looked behind the wheel of the old truck. After tugging gently on the fishing line they'd used to make sure the mannequin family wouldn't topple over, she headed for the truck's passenger side. Sunlight bathed Levi's grandparents' yard in a golden glow. She climbed inside and slammed the door.

"Okay, I'm ready. Finally."

"Let's do this." Levi shifted into gear, slowly tapped the accelerator, and eased the truck and trailer down the path toward the road.

Since she and her sisters had arrived at his grandparents' place early that morning, she'd worried her efforts may have been a waste of time. She had gone all out on the Denali-themed re-creation and probably tested the limits of Levi's dad's patience and the store's budget. But no matter how hard she tried, something still felt off about the float. Would she ever find the missing ingredient and make it as great as she wanted it to be? After all, a parade float couldn't get her a teaching job...or could it? Her imagination was on fire with ideas, yet at the same time, she felt terrible for pushing Levi's tolerance to the brink and exhausting her sisters. She had to try, though. This might be her only chance to stand out.

"You've done a fantastic job on this, Savvy." Levi glanced over at her with an approving smile.

"Thank you."

"It was really fun," she said, feeling warmth heat her skin as his praise settled into her bones. "Thanks for asking me."

"If they don't interview you for that teaching position after seeing this, then they don't know what's best for Opportunity High."

A blush rushed to her cheeks, and she ducked her head and looked away, trying to hide her embarrassment. "Hope you're right."

She'd obsessively checked both her email and her voice mail the last two days. No one had called to offer a job interview, though.

A few minutes later, they rolled down the side street in Opportunity, passing rows of clapboard houses that gave way to manicured green lawns before eventually leading to the designated spot for all the parade floats. As they approached their spot, gently wedged between two huge floats, Savannah tried to suppress her disappointment as she gazed at the sophisticated decorations adorning the tractor-trailer in front of them.

Levi's whistle broke the silence. "If that's the competition," he said, "you should have no problem winning the award for Most Creative."

His confidence contradicted her own thoughts. The thing was stunning. "Is that a real hot tub?"

"No." Levi squinted and leaned closer. "How could it be?"

Savannah sighed. "But that's Candace."

Right on cue, Candace glanced down from her perch beside the brilliant blue pool and waved.

They had streamers, balloons and at least a dozen inflatable beach balls. Had Candace persuaded her in-laws to tow an oversize bathtub down Main Street? Sure, they owned a hot tub business, but since when were tractor-trailers allowed on the parade route? People in Opportunity had always taken the Fourth of July parade very seriously, and Savannah remembered some incredible floats from her childhood years. But right now, all she could think about was how her balloon arch and hiking-in-Denali idea seemed so lackluster compared to the mobile pool-party theme Candace had come up with.

"Don't let her get under your skin," Levi said.

Savannah scoffed. "Um, too late. She's been getting under my skin since we were ten years old."

A smile tugged at his lips. He glanced at his

watch again. "The parents should be here with their kids any minute now."

"Is your mom bringing Wren over?"

"Yep." He drummed his thumb against the steering wheel. "Wren wouldn't miss this. Although we're going to have a hard time convincing her to throw the candy, because she's going to want to keep it for herself."

"Maybe the other kids tossing the candy will inspire her to go along with it." Savannah shifted to face him so she didn't have to watch Candace take yet another perfectly posed selfie.

"I'm still seeing her hoard food, Savvy," he said grimly.

"I know, but you're handling it well. We just have to keep making her feel like she's secure and loved."

A heavy silence descended on them both as they sat waiting in the truck.

Levi cleared his throat. "We're still doing this, right?"

"Pretending we're a thing?" She offered a bright smile. "Of course."

He winked. "Good."

Except she wasn't sure she was pretending anymore. The tenderness of his words stirred something inside her heart. A warmth spread through her chest at the thought of her and Levi and maybe even Wren becoming a family. Ridiculous, really. He'd never implied or asked for that level of commitment. Besides, Wren might eventually go back to live with her mother once she finished rehab. In a couple of weeks, Tori would leave town, and their charade would be over.

But none of those facts discouraged her from imagining a future that included Levi.

"You did it," Levi said, holding out his hand to Savannah for a high five. "I told you that your float was the best."

"It's *our* float." Savannah smacked his palm with her own, then shook her head in disbelief. "This wouldn't have happened without you and my sisters pitching in last minute."

Savannah had pulled off the impossible. After weeks of hard work, countless hours of planning and a long night of final touches, their float had been unanimously voted Most Creative. He'd had his doubts when they first joined the line at the start of the route. Especially when Candace got the kids riding on her float to launch those inflatable beach balls into the crowd.

"We made a pretty good team after all." Levi held up his phone. "Here, let me take a picture of you holding your award."

"Okay, but hurry. I'm starving," she said, tossing her head as a strand from her ponytail swept across her face.

He swiped to the camera and framed Savannah posing near the trailer's wheels.

She tipped her chin up and flashed another heart-stopping smile. Man, he could stand here for another twenty minutes taking her picture if she kept smiling like that.

"That's enough." She held out the plaque the Chamber of Commerce had awarded her. "Can you lock this in your truck for now?"

"Absolutely." He tucked his phone in his back jeans pocket, then unlocked the truck. Savannah opened the door and set the plaque on the front seat.

They rounded the back of the trailer and strode toward the festival booths lining Main Street. The midday sun wrapped them in warmth, and the smell of deep-fried food and sunscreen floated on the light breeze. On the makeshift stage nearby, a band played their opening song, a popular cover of a '90s hit. The crowd clapped and cheered.

Candace stepped into their path, the skirt of the pastel pink cover-up she'd donned over her swimsuit swirling around her legs.

Levi stifled a groan. The absolute last person he wanted to see right now.

"Oh no," Savvy grumbled.

Candace glared at Savannah as she spoke, her voice filled with disbelief. "Congrats on creating the most creative parade float, Savvy."

Savannah beamed with pride at Candace's congratulations. "You have to admit, it was pretty impressive."

"Yeah, you've been unstoppable lately. First, you catch the game-winning fly ball in softball, and now you've topped it off with the Most Creative Float of the Parade award. It almost makes me think that all your dreams are coming true." Candace's voice had a sharp edge to it as she continued. "Then there's your new boyfriend. A perfect triple crown of successes for our quirky little artist—or so it seems."

Levi slipped his arm around Savannah's shoulders and drew her close. "Come on, Candace. There's no need for you to be so negative."

But Candace wasn't backing down. She crossed her arms over her chest. "Oh, please, Levi, lighten up. Do you really think anyone believes this story you two have concocted?"

The air hung heavy between them until Levi responded. "You can think whatever you want. We know the truth."

Pressing up on her tiptoes, Savannah craned her neck to see around Candace. "By the way, your kid is about to put his fist through that cake over there."

"What? No—" Candace turned just in time to see her child slam his pudgy little hand into the middle of a gorgeous German chocolate cake that had been donated for the Key Club's cakewalk.

Savannah and Levi, relieved by the distraction, shared a quiet laugh. As Candace yelled at her son, they slipped away unnoticed.

"Perfect timing, kid. Perfect timing," Savannah said. "By the way, where's Wren?"

"The last time I saw her, your sisters were taking her to get her face painted. You don't think Candace saw through our act?" Levi asked skeptically.

Savannah bit her lip and shook her head. "What could she have seen that made her so suspicious?"

Levi stopped walking and tucked one of Savannah's stray strands of hair behind her ear. His expression softened as he cupped both hands around her face. "Maybe we haven't been putting enough of our feelings on display for everyone to see."

He leaned in closer and brushed his lips against hers ever so softly, drawing out the moment until she kissed him back. Time stood still as their mouths melded together. She tasted sweet, and when her hand closed around a fistful of his T-shirt, he longed to deepen the kiss. Reluctantly, he pulled away and looked into her now-gleaming eyes.

"This feels pretty real to me," she breathed out.

A slow smile spread across Levi's face despite the conflicting thoughts racing through his mind. He laced his fingers with hers. "Let's go find Wren."

Tori stepped into view, and Levi felt the familiar urge to look away when their eyes met. But this time, he held his gaze, squeezing Savannah's hand in reassurance. They moved toward the face-painting booth, where Wren proudly showed off the flower that now adorned her cheek.

"Wow," Levi said, admiring the bright yellow circle surrounded by pink petals outlined in light black lines. "You look amazing."

"That's so cool, Wren." Savannah looked at her sisters, who were standing beside the artist. "Good call, ladies."

They got cold drinks and a large tray of nachos, then wandered around until Wren got tired and asked to go home. Candace's hawk-eyed gaze had made its rounds, and he could feel the weight of her judgment every time she saw his and Savannah's fingers twined together. Part of him still wanted to stay and give the nosy woman a show. Wanted her and everyone else in Opportunity to know that he was grateful for Wren and Savannah, but he'd also learned not to push Wren beyond her limit.

Wren dropped her water bottle, and it splashed on the pavement, then rolled under a parked car. The little girl started to sob. As the tears slid down her cheeks and smudged her beloved painted flower, a hollow ache filled his chest.

So much for knowing when to call it quits.

Had he been too selfish? For all his griping about Jasper's impulsiveness, maybe his own need to control outcomes and pursue his perfect idea of a happy life had been equally problematic.

He stole a glance at Savannah as she scooped

Wren into her arms and quietly reassured her that they'd get more water. Levi halted his steps. To make things ten times worse, he'd gone and dragged sweet Savvy into his convoluted scheme, stealing kisses and persuading her to be his plus-one. An ominous feeling danced along his spine. What if this had all been a huge mistake? What if neither of them escaped this class reunion with their hearts intact?

"'This feels pretty real to me'?" Savannah shook her head in disbelief. "*Why* did I say that?"

"Maybe because it's the truth." Hayley swung her legs over the hot tub's edge, then slid into the water. "It's tough to fake a good kiss, don't you think?"

"You tell us," Juliet said from her perch in the opposite corner. "Who've you been kissing?"

"No one, lately." Hayley blushed. "How about we turn on the jets?"

She pushed a button on the control panel, and steam filled the air as their parents' hot tub motor churned up frothy bubbles.

"That's better," Juliet said. "My muscles are killing me."

"Same," Savannah said. This had been the longest Fourth of July ever. The faint scent of chlorine wafted toward Savannah's nostrils. She turned to Grace, her childhood bestie, who'd arrived from California yesterday. "I'm so glad this worked out for you to come over. We haven't seen each other since I visited you in California for New Year's Eve."

"Right." Grace's round face brightened with her flawless smile. "Can't believe it's been two years already. So, tell me everything. What have I missed?"

"I've applied for the art teacher position since Mr. Golden retired," Savannah said.

Grace's chocolate brown eyes grew wide. She paused, her plastic cup filled with strawberry lemonade halfway to her lips. "Hold up. You want to teach here? And what does that have to do with fake kisses? Because, by the way, I saw that kiss, and it was the opposite of fake."

"Oh, Grace." Hayley grinned. "We've missed you around here. You're not going to let Savvy get away with anything, are you?"

"Tell her, Savvy." Juliet twisted her hair into a bun on top of her head. "The whole complicated tale, from the beginning."

Savannah hesitated, fiddling with the straps on her one-piece swimsuit. Adrenaline hummed through her veins. The whole complicated tale? She wasn't quite ready to go there. Not until she had a job offer and a signed contract. There weren't three people she trusted more in the world than these women right here. But that didn't mean they needed to know *everything*.

"We'll start things off," Juliet said. "Savvy

agreed to help watch Levi Carter's foster kid, Wren."

Grace set her cup back in the holder. "Why?"

"Because he asked me to," Savannah said. "Also, I needed a summer job, and nothing else panned out."

"Wren's here temporarily, right?" Haley glanced at Savvy, seeking confirmation. "She'll be reunited with her mom later this summer?"

"That's a little tricky." Savannah splayed her fingers in the water in front of her. "Wren's mom is still in rehab in Anchorage."

"The point is, since Tori and Levi broke up, Levi is basically a single dad who needs reliable childcare," Juliet said. "Which is why he hired our sweet Savvy."

"Wait." Grace held up her hand. "Levi was engaged to Tori McCallister?"

"Uh-huh," Juliet said.

"But not anymore," Hayley added, waggling her eyebrows. "More on that in a minute."

"Oh my." Grace shook her head. "There are reality-TV shows with less drama than this."

"Where were we?" Juliet gave Savannah a questioning look.

"I'll take it from here," Savannah said. "Jasper and Mr. Carter hadn't made any plans to build a parade float, but they didn't want to skip the festival. So I said I'd babysit Wren part-time and handle design and decorations."

"I hope you charged double," Hayley said. "Because you sacrificed a lot of sleep for that float."

"If I don't have to deal with papier-mâché or use a hot-glue gun again this year, I'll be thrilled," Juliet said.

Savannah bit her lip. It hadn't occurred to her to ask for more money, not when Levi had mentioned their lack of funds.

"I'm guessing by your silence that they didn't offer a bonus." Sighing, Hayley reached for her can of soda. "Levi is fortunate to have you in his corner."

"Trying to keep up here, ladies," Grace said. "When do we get to the part about the not-fake kiss?"

"Back to the Tori and Levi subplot—" Juliet twisted the cap off her water bottle "—Tori broke up with Levi, and she's allegedly moving to Iowa later this summer for dental school. But we've seen her getting cozy with a guy who went to college with Jason's older brother and—"

"Easy, there, Nancy Drew." Hayley gently flicked water at Juliet. "We don't need to gossip about Tori."

"Ha, that's cute." Juliet shot Hayley a playful glare. "As if we aren't already gossiping plenty."

"These are straight facts," Savannah insisted. "Levi is not thrilled that she's still in town and casually dating somebody new, and he told me he didn't want to go to any reunion activities alone."

"So you agreed to be his date?" Grace's eyebrows sailed upward. "But I thought Jasper was the one you had a crush on."

"Jasper just proposed to Miranda," Juliet said.

"Argh." Grace tipped her head back. "Who's Miranda?"

Savannah and her sisters exchanged glances.

"She's a few years younger than us, just dropped out of college to be an influencer... That's really all we know." Savannah shrugged. "Anyway, between Jasper getting engaged and Tori ending theirs, Levi's been in a rough place emotionally."

"Can't blame him," Grace said. "I'd be crushed too."

"So, what's going on with the teaching job?" Hayley adjusted the buttons on the control panel again. "You said you applied, right?"

"I did apply, but no callback for an interview yet."

"You're not going back to Colorado, then?" Grace asked.

Savannah shook her head. "That job didn't work out."

"What about the guy you were seeing? Tim?"

"Troy," Savannah said. "We broke up."

Grace scrunched her nose. "Sorry to hear that. I thought you guys were really into each other."

"Yeah, I thought so too." Savannah glanced toward the firepit, where Dad and Wyatt had just brought out all the ingredients to make s'mores.

Maybe she should join them. Because she and Grace had been friends since fourth grade, there was very little they didn't know about each other's lives. Still, she wasn't ready to talk about the real reason why Troy broke up with her. Or why she'd moved home.

"If I don't hear something soon, I'm going to have to apply for something else." Savannah cast a look at the patio table, where she'd left her phone. If it was out of reach, then she couldn't refresh her email every few minutes. Waiting for an interview was driving her bananas.

Grace tapped at the ice in her cup with the straw. "Something else here?"

"No. Probably in Anchorage or Fairbanks. I thought about Orca Island. Hearts Bay High has a job open. I've always wanted to live there." Savannah forced a smile. "I'm up for an adventure."

"No, you can't move hundreds of miles away," Juliet said. "You just got here. Please don't stress. I'm sure Mr. Schubert will set up an interview with you soon."

"It's July fourth, Juliet." Savannah swiped at the moisture beading on her forehead. "School starts after Labor Day."

"That's plenty of time for them to hire someone," Hayley said.

"I hear what you're saying, but I have to be smart. There's no sense waiting around if they're not going to call."

"Give it just another day or two," Juliet said. "Mom and Dad will let you stay here a little bit longer if you need. No one's in a rush to get you to move on."

The back door opened, and their mom stepped out. "Hey, girls. Brought you some towels."

"Thanks," Juliet said. "Mom, tell Savannah she can live at home a little longer if she needs to."

Mom smiled. "Of course, dear. Your dad and I have enjoyed having you girls home this summer, and we are always happy to see Wyatt when he's not so busy with work. Are you concerned you're not going to get that job?"

"She's more concerned that she's falling in love." Juliet breathed out a swoony sigh. "I still don't get why that's a problem."

Mom pulled a deck chair up near the hot tub. "Tell me more."

"I can't." Grace splashed the water with her palm. "We're not doing another play-by-play of this whole hot mess."

"Here's the bottom line," Savannah said. "To try to make Tori jealous and to convince people that Levi and I are a couple, he kissed me twice in public."

"And it was a great kiss, apparently," Haley said. "I mean, from what we've been told."

Levi's words replayed in her head: *Shall I give myself ten out of ten stars?*

Her mouth twitched as she held back a smile.

"Great kisses. Both times. But that's the problem. What am I supposed to do when our relationship doesn't feel fake?"

Dad's and Wyatt's voices filtered into the evening air. The soothing water swirled around her weary body. She basked in the quiet comfort of having Mom, Hayley, Juliet and Grace surrounding her. It might have been exhaustion clouding her focus, but part of her remained unsettled.

She drew a fortifying breath and pressed a hand to her sternum. "When I agreed to this, I genuinely thought I was doing him a favor. Twice, he told me he only kissed me because he wanted our act to appear more convincing."

"Oh, wow. That's a challenge to maintain," Mom said. "Levi seems like a really great guy, and I admire what he's doing to take care of that little girl. I'm sure it isn't easy."

"Savvy, we've had fun teasing you tonight— but seriously, you have every right to look out for yourself." Hayley's eyes filled with concern. "Why don't you just tell him that this is getting too complicated and you need to step back?"

"There can't be too many more events left, right? What else does Candace have up her sleeve?" Grace asked.

"Only a formal dance at the Fairview." Savannah braced against the fiberglass bench and pushed herself up out of the water. The cool evening air enveloped her.

"Wow." Hayley shook her head. "She's really pulling out all the stops."

Savannah stood, her body protesting. She carefully stepped onto the deck and took the towel Mom handed her. Maybe Hayley was right. Maybe now was the best time to tell Levi they needed to rethink things. She'd still help with Wren, but tomorrow she'd start applying for teaching positions in other districts. Because she couldn't keep waiting around, hoping for an interview, wondering if Levi would ever risk his heart again.

Chapter Nine

If Wren's not thriving in your home, we can talk about transitioning her to a permanent placement elsewhere. But I have to be honest with you, Mr. Carter—that often has a negative impact on the child.

A negative impact? What did that even mean? He turned the social worker's words over and over, examining them from all angles as he followed Savannah into the Sluice Box. Conversation hummed, and laughter punctuated by the sound of the servers filling orders at the kitchen window washed over them in a gentle wave. A line snaked back from the hostess stand. Every chair in the cramped waiting area was occupied.

"Don't worry." Savannah offered him a smile that didn't quite reach her eyes. "Hayley said she'd hold a table for us."

"Cool. Thanks." Levi tucked his hands in his pockets and stood back, watching Savannah as she spoke to the hostess. The young woman nodded, grabbed two menus and motioned for them to follow her.

They threaded their way through the crowded dining room, with its rustic vaulted ceiling, well-loved dark wooden tables and chairs, high-back booths with red vinyl cushions, and his personal favorite—old mining paraphernalia propped up on display shelves. Framed vintage photos and newspaper clippings commemorated Opportunity's history during the Gold Rush.

The hostess stopped beside a cozy table in the back corner. How about that—his favorite. He'd always loved the old-school snowshoes mounted on the wall, positioned directly beneath an old miner's lamp hanging from one of the high beams and above a photo of Denali on a perfect summer day, with gorgeous purple lupine blooming in the meadow.

On the opposite side of the dining room, Hayley stood next to a rowdy table full of climbers, her pen hovering over her notepad. They looked to be celebrating a successful expedition on the mountain. Max Butler sat at the end of the table, with sunburned skin, tousled blond hair and a scraggly beard. But it was the light in his eyes and the look on his face when he glanced up at Hayley and smiled that gave Levi pause. What was going on there?

None of your business, Carter. Grab a seat.

"This is a table for four." Savannah hesitated.

"There's just the two of us. Are you sure you don't mind?"

"It's the only table I have left. Unless you want to wait an hour," the hostess said. "You're Hayley's sister, right?"

Savannah nodded.

"Then don't worry about it. We're like family around here." She patted the worn surface with her palm. "Enjoy."

Savannah sat down.

Levi settled into the chair opposite hers. He couldn't help but admire her hair, cascading in glossy curls over her exposed shoulders. She wore a dainty blue sundress dotted with white flowers, its narrow straps highlighting her delicate collarbone.

She set her bag on the chair next to her and opened up the menu. "What do you usually get when you come here?"

He was ready to answer with his go-to order of turkey-bacon club, but then he noticed her smooth porcelain skin and full pink lips. Man, he'd been an idiot thinking he could pretend to date her without wanting an authentic relationship. These feelings and emotions were so unexpected, though. Maybe it was the way she cared for Wren. Or made him laugh.

Could he jump back into a relationship? What if he wasn't ready? Besides, he wasn't real sure she was ready either.

"Levi?" Savannah dipped her head and forced him to make eye contact. "Everything all right?"

He shook his head as if to clear the fog. "Yeah, I'm fine. Had a really intense meeting with Wren's social worker today. Do you think you could help me sort out what she said?"

"Of course." Her pale eyebrows knitted together. "But I need to tell you something."

Before either could go on, their server came and took their order, leaving them in an awkward silence.

"What did the social worker have to say?" Savvy asked as she leaned forward in her chair.

"No, you go first. What's on your mind?"

A deep sigh escaped her lips as she met Levi's gaze. "I think we should end this charade. It's getting too complicated."

Her words pierced him. "What? Why?"

"I still don't have a permanent job, so who knows if I'll even be here much longer." She picked at the paper wrapper encircling her napkin and utensils. "Somebody's bound to get hurt. And what will people think when they find out we've been faking this?"

"There they are." Alexis paused beside the table where Levi and Savvy sat. "I have to say, y'all are just the cutest couple. David and I have been talking about how perfect you look together."

"Hashtag couple goals." David grinned, draping his arm around Alexis's shoulders. "Hey, would you guys mind if we joined you? This place is packed."

"Unless this is date night," Alexis added, feigning a grimace. "We don't want to interrupt your time together."

Stalling, Levi swiveled his gaze to meet Savannah's. "See that, babe? Other people want to be like us."

Savvy gave almost an imperceptible shake of her head.

Regret tightened like a fist in his gut.

Maybe she was right. This was getting out of hand. At first, he'd wanted someone at his side for the reunion activities so he wouldn't have to go alone. He'd hoped Savvy's presence would spare him pitiful glances and his mother's nagging. But if he was honest, part of him had enjoyed seeing Tori's reaction as well. Maybe his plan to make Tori feel bad was going to backfire and make Savvy feel worse. And maybe a goal of making someone feel bad wasn't a good goal at all.

"Actually," he said, surprising himself, "we were just talking about something important. We'll catch up later."

"Sure, yeah. No worries." Alexis and David both looked confused, but they took the hint and left.

Levi took a deep breath. "Look, I don't want to shut this down. I know it's complicated, and maybe it's ridiculous, but…" He trailed off, unsure of how to proceed.

"But what?"

"I need you. Your help. With Wren, I mean." His skin heated as he fumbled over his words.

Savannah's eyes widened. The muffled sound of her phone ringing drew her attention toward her purse.

Please don't answer that, he silently pleaded.

"That might be the call I'm expecting." She wrinkled her nose. "Sorry."

"Not a problem. Go ahead."

She pulled her phone from her bag, glanced at the screen and then sucked in a breath. "I'm going to take this outside."

Before he could respond, their server arrived with drinks, a basket of pretzel bites and cheese sauce, and a stack of napkins. "Here you go. Enjoy."

"Thanks." Levi unwrapped his straw as Savvy slid out from her seat and walked away, her phone pressed to her ear.

Savory aromas wafted in the air, making his stomach growl. He eyed the food in the basket on the table. He'd wait for Savvy. Hopefully, she wouldn't be too much longer. Raucous laughter spilled from the booth behind him. Sipping his soda, he bounced his knee up and down beneath the table. Worst-case scenarios spooled through his head. What if she couldn't find a job here and decided to move away?

A few minutes later, she reclaimed her spot across from him, her cheeks flushed pink and her eyes bright.

"You look happy. Good news?"

Grinning, she tore the wrapper from her straw and dropped it into her soda. "I have an interview on Friday morning with Mr. Schubert."

Hope took flight in his chest. "Wow, that's great. Congratulations." He lifted his glass and tipped the rim against hers. "You're a perfect fit for the job."

Her smile dimmed. "I don't know about that, but I'm super relieved he finally called."

"I don't think you have anything to worry about."

She dipped her chin, spread her napkin on her lap and then plated a pretzel bite. "I appreciate your kind words. Now, where were we?"

His heart hammered. "I was telling you how much I need your help."

She hesitated, the small bowl of cheese sauce suspended over her plate. "We don't have to be 'dating' for me to keep helping you with Wren, though."

"True." He frowned. "Can we stick this out until after the dance at the Fairview? Please?"

Savannah quirked her mouth to one side. "All right—but then we're staging a dramatic breakup or something because I can't keep this up much longer."

"Perfect." He smiled in a desperate attempt to mask his disappointment. The dance was only three days away. That meant he had seventy-two hours to craft a plan, and find the courage, to tell her how he truly felt.

Opportunity's historic Fairview Hotel had never looked more stunning. Patriotic bunting festooned the porch railings; strands of white lights encircled the cottonwood trees flanking the wide wooden steps; and red, white and blue pansies spilled from freshly painted window boxes. The glorious old structure that had once served as a boarding house for weary prospectors looked eager to receive Savannah and her classmates.

"Let me get your door," Levi said as he stepped out of his car. His eyes met hers as he walked around to her side and opened the passenger door. She adjusted her long yellow gown, the fabric rustling softly under her newly manicured fingertips. Carefully, she placed one dainty heel onto the gravel and then the other, already regretting her choice of footwear.

Levi's gentlemanly gesture of opening the car door for her roused an uneasy feeling in her stomach. Despite her insistence the other night at the Sluice Box that they call this whole thing off, she couldn't help but wonder how she'd ever go back to being officially single. He'd been so sweet. So attentive. And those kisses… She wobbled, and Levi clasped her elbow, his fingers warm on her bare skin.

"Everything okay?"

"Yeah." She managed a nervous smile. "Borrowed shoes, and all that."

Levi's gaze swept from her toes to the top of her head, lingering when their gaze met.

"You look beautiful, Savannah," he said softly.

A warm blush heated her neck and spread to her cheeks. "Thank you," she said. "You look handsome."

He glanced down at his crisp white dress shirt, striped tie, deep navy slacks and caramel brown dress shoes. "Thanks. Jasper helped me out."

"What does it say about us that we needed our siblings to help us get dressed for this?"

"It says they have great taste. Come on, let's dance the night away."

"Oh, on second thought, let's go roast marshmallows in my parents' yard."

"Not so fast." His fingers trailed down her arm and laced with hers, leaving a pleasant, tingling sensation on her skin. "We have a fake relationship to maintain, remember?"

The question, even with a hint of humor clinging to his words, made her smile falter. She'd miss him when they parted ways.

"We're going to have to dance at least three

slow songs just to keep up our facade," he added, winking.

She tucked her hand into his outstretched elbow. "I'm in."

The truth was, as much as dancing made her self-conscious, and even though she already regretted letting her sisters talk her into these heels, she had daydreamed about how swaying in Levi's arms would feel. Savannah snuck a glance at Levi as they made their way to the entrance of the grand hotel. Gently, he guided her up the stairs. The door opened, and they stepped into a room filled with people dressed in their finest. A band hired from out of town filled the air with live music as servers circulated among the guests, offering drinks and hors d'oeuvres.

Levi ran a trembling hand down the length of his striped tie as he hesitated outside the ballroom.

Was he nervous too? She avoided meeting his gaze, gulped down her apprehension and let him lead her into the grand hall. The room swelled with the sound of music and chatter as friends and former teachers reconnected. Savannah spotted Grace standing next to her date, waiting to have their pictures taken at the photo booth. She waved, then followed Levi onto the crowded dance floor.

Buoyed by the success of her job interview for the art teacher position and the warmth in Levi's liquid brown eyes as they danced together, she shoved aside her lingering worries about her future. When the band took a break, she and Levi meandered outside. The air was crisp and cool on their skin. They walked onto the balcony, which overlooked a small courtyard surrounded by trees and blooming flowers. Sunlight glinted off the water as it splashed playfully from the ornate fountain at the intersection of two flagstone paths. The sky overhead held breathtaking streaks of pale pink and orange.

Yet despite the seemingly perfect moment, an unease drifted around them.

"Want something to drink?" Levi offered, turning to face her.

"Water would be great," she said. "Thank you."

"Be right back." He squeezed her arm gently and offered a tender smile. But before he left the balcony, Candace and Mr. Schubert stormed out of the ballroom, blocking the doorway.

"There she is." Candace held her phone in one hand and pointed at Savannah with the other. "I've shared some information with Mr. Schubert that I think might interest you."

Savannah's mouth went dry. "I doubt it."

Mr. Schubert's uncomfortable expression made her wince. The man looked as if he'd rather be anywhere else but here, a feeling she was beginning to share. She dug her fingernails into her palms. Levi returned to her side, grabbing the railing behind him with both hands.

"I have some connections in Colorado," Candace continued. "My cousin is dating a teacher named Troy. When he found out she had family here in Opportunity, he shared some troubling news today that I feel bears repeating."

"I'm sure you do," Levi muttered.

"The tragic events revealed to me confirm what I've suspected." Candace tipped up her chin. "Savannah's been lying since she got here."

Candace's statement sent Savannah's heart rate into overdrive. Her chest tightened. Sweat trickled down her spine. But she managed to find her voice.

"What are you talking about, Candace?"

Candace smirked with a flinty gleam in her eyes. "Oh, please. Don't play dumb. Did you really think the truth wouldn't follow you back home?"

"I didn't—"

"You shouldn't be allowed anywhere near children," Candace insisted, her voice getting louder and drowning out Savannah's protests.

"No crime was committed," Savannah said. She quickly scanned the group fanning out around them, nothing but shock and dismay reflected on their faces.

Candace planted her hands on her hips. "You lost your job because a kid *died*. That's something that this community needs to know about."

"It wasn't my fault," Savannah whispered. The disapproval emanated through the crowd in waves. Had Levi just taken a noticeable step away, or was that her imagination?

The principal's brow furrowed. "Savannah," he said softly, "that's the kind of information you need to disclose in an interview."

"No, it isn't." She squeezed the words past her tight throat. "It was a church youth trip, and I was a volunteer chaperone. The kid—"

"The details hardly matter at this point," Candace said. "The outcome is still the same—a family lost their beautiful teenage daughter because of you."

Savannah flinched. "But that's not the whole story."

Oh, how she hated the desperate tone in her voice. "Please, Mr. Schubert, you have to believe me. Please just let me tell you what really happened."

"It's a little late for that," he said. "You omitted important information, which is something we usually deem a deal-breaker. I'm going to have to consider withdrawing your name from the art teacher–applicant pool. I'll send you confirmation of my decision in writing."

"Please, no." Tears pressed against the back of her eyes. "You have to believe me. I wasn't responsible for the child's actions."

"Miss Morgan, I'm not about to rehash that story with you now. My main concern is you neglected to tell us something that would have caused considerable unease if it had surfaced after you were on board." Anger and disappointment flashed in the man's eyes. "Perhaps in the future, you should consider telling the truth. All of it."

Savannah swallowed against the sour taste climbing the back of her throat. Then she turned and faced Levi. The pain in his eyes was almost unbearable to see.

"You believe me, right?"

He swallowed hard.

"Levi?" She stepped closer. "You know I'd never intentionally harm a child. Haven't I shown you that I'm more than capable of taking care of Wren?"

"I—I'd have believed you if you'd given me the chance. But you didn't tell me about this... incident. A girl's death, Savannah. A girl under your care. Like Wren..." He swallowed again and stared into the distance. "Why did you hide it— because you knew I'd find it troubling?" he said.

He looked as if he were seeing her for the first time and not liking the image she presented. She could see the doubt and anger in his eyes, and it crushed her.

"I want to believe you. I do, Savannah. I want to hear your side of the story, but I can't right now. I think it would be best if we had some space."

Space. Right. A sob rose in her throat. She turned and fled the balcony. Her skin burned with shame. Why didn't anyone believe her? How had Candace managed to turn everyone against her in a matter of minutes?

"Why isn't Sabby coming over?" Wren stared up at Levi, her little hands clamped onto the front windowsill.

The confusion in the little girl's eyes nearly made him crumble. Levi glanced at the driveway, half wishing Savannah was pulling in right now. Toting a bag full of kid-friendly activities and Wren's favorite snacks. But that couldn't happen. He had to think of Wren's safety first. The scandalous news that had broke at the Fairview last night indicated that Savannah hadn't been completely honest about her employment history. That could affect his ability to keep Wren, if the social worker found out he'd not done a good-enough job vetting a babysitter.

Or had Candace made this all up?

He shoved the idea aside. Candace enjoyed being in the thick of the drama, but she didn't have the capability to manufacture false information about Savannah's life in Colorado, right?

His head spun. Wren tugged on his hand, bringing him back to reality. He had to find a way to figure this all out.

A red Jeep turned down the road. *Oh no.* The vehicle slowed to a stop, then eased into his driveway.

Wren gasped. "Is that Sabby in a new car?"

"No, sweetie. That's Tori. She used to be my... girlfriend."

"Oh. Is Sabby your girlfriend?"

"Not anymore."

Wren quirked her lips to one side. "That's sad. No girlfriends."

You're telling me.

Despite the knot in his gut as Tori climbed out of her Jeep and walked toward his front door, he couldn't help but smile at how Wren could make him forget about his worries with just one observation or phrase or laugh. She was already making him a better person than he had ever been before on his own.

"Wren, I'm going to speak with Tori outside. Do you think you could sit quietly on the couch and watch a movie while I step onto the porch?"

Wren nodded emphatically. "Yes."

He leaned down and pulled her in for a hug. "You are a very sweet girl. Did you know that?"

She squirmed out of his embrace and tried to hide her smile. "Yeah, I know."

Wren started toward the couch but then suddenly turned and ran back to throw her arms around him again to give him another hug.

"Thank you," he whispered as she pulled away.

Tori knocked softly.

His heart kicked against his ribs. What could she possibly want? They'd said everything they needed to say months ago. "I'll get your movie started in a second. Hang on."

He straightened, then turned and opened the door. "Hello, Tori. What are you doing here?"

"Hi, Levi." She smiled. Her sable hair moved softly in the wind, and her deep green eyes bored into his. "Can I come in?"

He shook his head. "No, you can't," he said gently. "But if you'll wait, I'll be with you shortly."

Pain crossed her expression before she nodded and stepped away. Levi closed the door, feeling a heaviness he couldn't explain sink inside him. The dramatic events at the dance still felt so fresh, and now here was Tori, of all people, throwing Levi off-balance.

He helped Wren get some popcorn and more water in her bottle, then queued up an animated movie. "I'll be right outside if you need me, okay?"

Wren pulled her pink-and-white blanket over her lap and settled in with her bowl of popcorn. "I'm fine, thank you."

Wow. So polite. Savvy would be impressed. His lungs locked at the thought of all the things he wouldn't get to tell Savannah. She wouldn't be here to see Wren start school or watch her learn to read or hear all about the friends Wren made at preschool.

He palmed the back of his neck. Man, it had been less than twenty-four hours since all the drama at the Fairview, and he already couldn't stand the hole that Savannah's absence had left in his life. Drawing a deep breath, he opened the door and stepped outside.

Tori waited at the bottom of the steps. The wind rustled the leaves on the trees and blew her hair across her face. She turned and stared at him with a sad smile on her face. "Is Wren okay?"

"She will be." He leaned against the railing and crossed his arms over his chest. "What's up?"

"I came to say goodbye again."

"Pretty sure we covered that when you called off our engagement."

She looked down and dragged the toe of her sandal through the gravel on his walkway. "I know, and I'm sorry that things didn't work out between us, Levi. I have a confession to make. Something that might make this hard for both of us."

He scoffed. "Haven't heard enough salacious news lately. Go ahead. Lay it on me."

Tori's sheepish gaze found his. "I was super jealous when I saw you with Savannah."

He swallowed hard. "Really."

She nodded.

He dragged his fingertips across his jaw. At one time, he had thought those words would bring sweet satisfaction. After all, inciting jealousy had been his plan, as juvenile as it was.

"There were a couple of times when I thought

about saying something. Telling you that it wasn't fair that you'd moved on so fast."

He shifted his weight from one foot to the other. "You showed up with a date to all the reunion events too."

"I know. That was just a casual thing. He didn't stick around. Besides, I'm still moving to Iowa."

Frustration bubbled in his veins. "So why are you here?"

"I just wanted to tell you that I saw a look in your eyes when you and Savannah were together that I had never seen you give me. I know people have been talking behind your backs, and you didn't ask for my advice, but I think you should fight for her. That's why I came here."

His frustration morphed into anger. Tori had broken his heart, and now she thought she could waltz on by and try to mend it again by pushing him toward Savannah. That was cheap restitution, and he wasn't buying it. Besides, he'd just felt betrayed by Savannah, too, so reconciling with her wasn't happening, no matter what Tori thought she was doing. He wouldn't let her continue this mission of mercy. It didn't feel sincere. "You're right. I wasn't looking for your input. Thanks for stopping by, and I wish you well. I'm sure you're going to be an excellent dentist."

He turned, went back inside his house and heard her Jeep pulling away in just a few seconds.

"Want to watch this moobie with me?" Wren asked, peering at him over the couch cushions.

"You know it. What did I miss?" He plopped down beside her.

She handed him the remnants of her popcorn. "Here, I'll share."

"Thanks." He set the bowl in his lap. As the movie played and Wren explained the opening scene, he tried to focus, but Tori's words kept looping through his mind.

Was she right? Did he need to go after Savannah? How could he ever trust her again after the secret she'd kept?

Chapter Ten

Choking back another sob, Savannah crossed over to the dresser, pulled open the bottom drawer and scooped out her jeans. If she hurried, she could catch the southbound train passing through Opportunity on its way from Fairbanks to Anchorage. She'd have to fork out some cash for the ticket, plus a hotel room. Maybe the news about her scandal hadn't spread far yet and she'd be able to connect with a friend to room with. At least until she had a decent job.

After dropping more clothes into the open suitcase on the bottom bunk, she returned to the closet, pushing aside her sisters' clothing until she found her own tops. Hayley and Juliet had probably borrowed one or two of her outfits, but she didn't have time to worry about that now. She shoved the rest of her clothes into the suitcase without bothering to fold anything. Another decision she'd regret later. Right now she was too upset to care. She took her dirty clothes out of the laundry basket and shoved them into a plastic shopping bag she'd found under the bed.

Peeking under the bed had reminded her of Wren and the substantial number of snacks she'd had squirreled away. Savannah meant to remind Levi to follow up on the hoarding tendencies with the social worker. It had slipped her mind. Her chest ached at the reminder of how she'd been plucked from Wren's life like a salmon snatched from the river by a hungry bear.

Poor Wren. She'd endured so much loss and instability already. Just when they were getting attached, Savannah's past had come roaring back to bite them both. She glanced around the bedroom, taking one last look at the place. She'd miss rooming with her sisters, staying up late and teasing one another. But she couldn't stay here, not anymore. Her heart was too shattered. She couldn't handle being in the same place as Levi.

There were footsteps outside her door, and she took a deep breath, trying to calm herself down. When her mother poked her head in, Savannah forced a smile. "Hey, Mom."

Her attempt to sound cheerful fell flat.

Mom's eyes narrowed as she took in Savannah's suitcase and duffel bag. "What's going on, honey? Why are you packing?"

"I'm leaving."

"Wait. What are you doing?" Hayley came into the room with Juliet close behind.

"Leaving?" Juliet pushed past Mom and Hayley, shock etched on her features. "Why?"

Savannah unplugged her charging cable from the wall, twisted the cord and took a deep breath, trying to keep her voice steady. "What do you mean, 'why'? You know what happened."

Her mother stepped farther into the room and pulled Savannah into a tight hug. "Sweetie, I know it hurts right now, but you don't have to move on."

"Everyone in town thinks I'm a liar and a murderer." Savannah gulped back another sob as she sagged against Mom's shoulder.

"That's a bit of an exaggeration," Juliet said calmly. "Unless there's something more that you're not telling us?"

Savannah stepped away from her mother and swallowed hard before confessing. "I did lose my job," she whispered. "That part is true—but I didn't hurt anyone."

Hayley and Juliet came closer, their faces filled with warmth and sympathy.

"I was chaperoning," Savannah continued, her voice shaking slightly. "A church youth-group thing. They asked me to come along because they knew I had experience skiing. So I said yes." She paused, taking a deep breath before explaining further. "I was in charge of a group of teenagers, and one snuck out after lights-out. She went skiing where she wasn't supposed to and then…she fell into a hole in the snow at the base of a tree. By the time they found her, it was too late."

Her sisters gasped.

"That's terrible," Hayley murmured. "But why did they blame you?"

Savannah sighed. "Because of angry parents and a group of vocal people who thought their kids should have been watched more closely," she said. "We didn't post guards on them all night like they were prisoners. They knew what the rules were. They weren't children. Sadly, she paid for breaking those rules with her life."

"Oh, honey. You should have told us. It wasn't your fault. Maybe this will all blow over soon," Mom said, folding Savannah's quilt and neatly stacking it at the end of the bed.

"Not if Candace is involved." Savannah slipped her hoodie over her head. "I don't know why she felt obligated to share my past mistakes with Mr. Schubert and all of Opportunity. I never talked about it much because the girl was at fault, and I didn't think it right to spill the story of her tragic mistake everywhere I went. There's nothing I can do except move and start over. Again. Because I sure don't belong here."

Mom's eyes filled with tears. "That is not true. Of course you belong here."

"I'm done fighting for something that isn't meant to be," Savannah said. "I can't take the small-town nosiness any longer."

"You don't have to do this," Juliet insisted. "I know it's hard, but you can stay here and find another job—or at least try to work things out with Levi."

Savannah shook her head. "No, it's too late for that. Everyone in town thinks I'm guilty of something I didn't do, and Levi sided with them."

"So where are you going to go?" Hayley asked.

Savannah shrugged. "I need a fresh start somewhere else. Somewhere new where people don't have any preconceived notions of who I am or what kind of person I am. Maybe Fiji? Or Honolulu? Maybe I'll finally take that gap year in Europe like I always dreamed of."

Juliet shot her a disbelieving look. "You're really just going to buy a one-way ticket and completely walk away?" she asked, her voice cracking. "What about Wren?"

"I'll miss Wren dearly," Savannah said, as the tears kept coming. What would Levi tell Wren about her now that everyone had already made up their minds without listening to her story first?

Hayley grabbed her arm gently. "Just give it some time, please. Don't do anything rash. Like Mom said, maybe this will blow over in a few days."

Savannah bit back a snide remark and turned away. "I told you, folks have already decided for themselves what they want to believe." She made space in the suitcase for her flip-flops and her hiking boots, then yanked the zipper closed. "The school district will never hire me now. And without a job, I can't afford to stay here."

With her heart aching, she stood her suitcase on its wheels, stacked her duffel bag on top and then forced a brave smile. "Who wants to drive me to the train station?"

Levi loaded two more boxes of energy bars onto the hand truck and toted them off the loading dock and into the stockroom at the back of the store. He added them to the shelves, noted their quantity and their arrival date on his clipboard, then returned to the loading dock. The driver of the delivery truck added three more boxes of apparel to the stack before passing him the tablet.

"That's the last of your order on this shipment, sir."

"Thanks, man." Levi quickly scrawled a signature on the digital tablet, then handed it back. "See you next time. Safe travels."

"Sure thing." The guy tucked his tablet under his arm, slammed the door on the back of his truck, then jogged to the driver's side and hopped inside. A few minutes later, he beeped the horn before pulling away.

Levi loaded the first box of clothing onto the hand truck and turned toward the store. Jasper blocked his path.

Oy. "Excuse me. I have work to do."

"Come on, man." Jasper braced his hands on his hips. "Don't be like this. I just want to talk."

Levi sighed and tried to keep his patience in check. Jasper had been bugging him all week, and he was getting fed up with it. He had work to do and no time for chitchat with family—especially not right now, when he was running late for a meeting with one of the vendors.

When Jasper didn't budge, Levi gritted his teeth, angled the hand truck around his twin and wheeled the load toward the store's back door.

"Why aren't you answering my texts?" Jasper called after him.

"Simple—I don't want to talk to you."

Jasper followed him into the storeroom. When Levi stopped the hand truck, Jasper grabbed the first box and shoved it into an opening on the bottom shelf.

"Wait. I have to inventory those."

"So inventory them." Jasper shrugged. "We can talk while you work."

"In case you missed it, I don't have anything to say." Levi grabbed his clipboard and marked off the long-sleeve shirts and T-shirts from his list.

Jasper watched silently as Levi worked. He seemed to be searching for words, but he didn't speak until Levi had placed the last item on its shelf.

Finally, he cleared his throat. "Look, I know

you're upset and you think that what Savannah did was wrong. But I—"

"What she did *is* wrong," Levi said. "I'm still trying to figure out what—or if—I should tell the social worker about this. Hiring a babysitter who had a student's death in her past."

"And I don't want you to get any angrier than you already are—"

"Jasper, no." Levi threw his pen and his clipboard down on top of a stack of cardboard boxes and shoved his fingers through his hair. "What have you done?"

"I did some background investigating." Jasper stepped back with both palms held up in self-defense. "Hear me out, please. If Candace can make calls to Colorado, then so can I."

Levi's scalp prickled. "And what did you discover?"

"That maybe Savannah doesn't deserve to have people piling on her. She was an innocent bystander in a terrible tragedy."

"Oh, here we go." Levi shook his head in disbelief and reached for the hand truck. "To hear Candace tell it—and from the newspaper articles I found online—someone's dead. It seems to me that Savannah didn't mention any of that before I put her in charge of Wren. That's a pretty important detail to leave out. So she lied, Jasper."

Jasper bit his lip and nodded slowly, his expression guarded yet sympathetic. "She wasn't technically lying—she wasn't there when the accident happened, so she can't be blamed for anything that occurred. But yeah, she should've told you everything up front instead of trying to minimize her involvement. I still think you're being way too hard on her."

He paused, maybe to give Levi a moment to consider his words. "The thing is, bad things happen to good people sometimes—we just have to figure out how to deal with them the best way we can."

Levi didn't answer at first. He just stared at his twin before finally taking a deep breath. "I want to believe you, but until she can prove it by her actions instead of just words..." He trailed off and shook his head. "I'm not sure if I ever will be able to trust her again."

Jasper pinned him with a long look. "People will often disappoint you, bro."

Levi opened his mouth to speak, but Jasper cut him off with an emphatic shake of his head. "I know you don't want to hear it, but I think it might actually be beneficial for both of you if you took a step back and tried to understand what Savannah went through before passing judgment."

Levi sighed heavily and crossed his arms. He knew Jasper was right, that maybe he had been too quick to judge, but he still couldn't shake the hurt. Savannah could've just been honest, and they would've avoided this whole mess.

Like you were honest about your relationship?

Guilt swept in. He shook his head, suddenly feeling very drained. "Okay, so what do you suggest I do?"

Jasper shrugged. "It's up to you, obviously, but maybe try talking with her about it? Just give her time to explain herself, and then go from there."

Levi nodded slowly as he considered this advice. He wasn't proud of how he'd behaved. He'd let himself get swept up in the drama. Assumed the worst. Admitting Jasper had a valid point wasn't easy, but if he didn't listen, he'd always regret letting pride keep him and Savvy apart.

Jasper's phone hummed. He plucked it from his back pocket, then frowned as he scanned the screen. "'This is a text from Hayley. Savannah's at the train station. She's headed for Anchorage. Train leaves in eight minutes.'"

Levi's heart sank. Savvy couldn't leave. Not now. Not like this. He had to try to stop her.

Savannah stifled a sob as the train whistle blew, bringing back the memories of all she was leaving behind. She settled in her seat and pressed her forehead against the cool glass, trying to dredge up the strength to get through this journey as tears ran silently down her cheeks. She'd been so foolish, still clinging to her silly notion that Levi would come for her, running through the station to stop the train from departing before it was too late. Through tear-filled eyes, she frantically searched the platform and the parking lot one last time but found no trace of him or his beloved truck. Her heart broke as she realized she and Wren hadn't officially said goodbye.

The pain was almost too much to bear.

Why had she ever believed she could keep her past hidden? That no one would discover the catastrophic mistakes she'd made in Colorado? Her job loss and the fallout from her community and her employer had left a mark. Even her ex, Troy, had managed to get one last dig in by using his new girlfriend to spread the word about the accident. And now all that pain had come rushing back like water breaching a dam. It was the same hurt all over again. Crushing her until she could barely breathe. Looming over all of it was the sorrow and grief she'd experienced at the loss of a girl under her care. She'd struggled to make sense of it, to find comfort, but sometimes she felt she didn't deserve it when the student's family was suffering so much more.

As much as she didn't want to leave Opportunity, she couldn't stay. It wasn't just the lack of a steady job that propelled her to leave—she'd never be able to handle the ridicule. Candace would have a field day, tormenting her with reminders of her failure.

The train whistle blew one more time, and then, moments later, her car started rolling down the tracks. She couldn't take in the full scope of the beauty around her, not after she'd just said good-bye to everyone and everything she had loved here. Before the station disappeared from view, she glanced over her shoulder for a last look at the platform, hoping that someone would come sprinting after her. But no one did. No matter how hard she tried to stop them, the tears kept coming as the train picked up speed. She was leaving all her dreams and hopes behind, moving to a big city with no one waiting for her arrival. It all felt so pointless now.

She had worked hard to make sure the youth-group incident was hidden from view when she applied for the job in Opportunity. And while it had pained her deeply to conceal such big parts of herself—her mistakes and failures—she knew it was necessary if she wanted a fresh start. How would she have covered it, anyway? *Oh, by the way, Mr. Schubert, you should know that when I was chaperoning a field trip, a girl died.* She'd wrestled with whether to reveal it but in the end decided she needed to put it behind her if she was to accept she wasn't to blame.

But somehow, here on this train, with only her thoughts for company, all the memories and pain she'd been trying to avoid replayed in her mind. Forced her to second-guess her choices. Savannah hugged her knees close to her chest as she wept silently, feeling more alone than ever before. She hadn't expected it to be so hard leaving everything behind.

"Honey, are you okay?"

Savannah turned from the window to see a woman seated across from her. She had silver hair twisted into a no-nonsense bun, plenty of laugh lines fading out from her kind blue eyes. Savvy couldn't help but like the woman's warm presence instantly. Savannah dabbed away at the tears that still threatened to fall. "I'm all right."

The woman nodded slowly and then motioned for Savannah to draw closer. Hesitantly, she moved forward until she was close enough for the woman to take her hand and give it a gentle squeeze.

"My name is Martha, and wherever you're going on this train, you can tell me about it."

Savvy didn't know what to say at first. She had been doing her best not to think about what she'd do for work or where exactly she was headed after she got to Anchorage—mainly because she hadn't decided yet. All her talk about Fiji and Honolulu or backpacking in Europe had been nonsense. Because she couldn't afford any of that.

But as Martha waited patiently for an answer, Savannah spilled everything out to her new companion: how she'd lost her job in Colorado due to an unfortunate incident involving a student who'd disobeyed the rules, how that same incident had come back around again in Opportunity thanks to

Candace's power of persuasion. How much it hurt that even after all these months, the pain was still so raw and real, and how now Levi knew more than he should ever know about her past.

The kind stranger continued to listen without interrupting as the words tumbled out until Savannah fell silent again. Exhaustion made every limb feel like it weighed about a thousand pounds. But she also felt strangely relieved now that someone else knew her story too.

"It's just that…" She drew another wobbly breath. "I thought I had my happily-ever-after, you know? After some fits and starts, I thought he was maybe the one."

When she finished speaking, Martha gave Savannah's hand another reassuring squeeze.

Then she shifted in her seat. "Well, maybe he is and just needs a little time to figure it all out."

"Oh, I doubt that's going to happen. He's made his choice."

"Here's what I can say for certain. God's timing is nothing like ours. I'm sure you know that. Sometimes, when you are just at your wit's end, He has a way of bringing the good stuff back around."

Savvy sighed again. "I know that, but it's so hard to hold on to the hope. I look around and I see all these happy couples, like my parents, and I wonder why it's not like that for me."

Martha smiled sympathetically. "Bless their

hearts—but you can't compare your journey to anyone else's. God has a plan for you."

Savannah nodded slowly and tried to take comfort in Martha's words. As the train chugged along the track, they passed endless fields of wild-flowers in full bloom and caught an occasional glimpse of a mama moose and her babies eating at the edge of a pond.

The picturesque scenes were a comforting reminder that God had His own ways of doing things and that she didn't just get whatever she wanted. She'd accepted long ago that He was in control. But it still didn't ease the pain.

"Can't you drive any faster?" Levi rubbed his damp palms on his jeans, then glanced at the clock on the dash. "The train gets into Anchorage soon. I don't want to miss her."

Jasper, with his hands at a white-knuckle grip of ten and two, kept a steady speed. "I'm trying to obey the law. If I get pulled over for speeding it'll take us even longer to get there. Is that what you want?"

Levi gritted his teeth in despair as he watched the speedometer's needle remain stuck at sixty miles an hour. "So today's the day you conveniently decide not to have a lead foot. Cool."

"Do you want me to just turn around and go back home so you can do this yourself?"

"No, I want you to hurry up so I can make

things right," Levi growled. "Like you said I was supposed to. Remember?"

Jasper pressed his foot on the gas pedal, then abruptly slammed on the brakes and pulled over to the side of the road. Gravel kicked out from under the tires as his truck lurched onto the shoulder.

Levi dug his fingers into the armrests. "What's going on? Why did you pull over?"

Jasper stopped the truck, shifted into Park, then killed the engine and turned to face Levi with a fierce intensity in his expression. A muscle twitched in his jaw as he stared straight ahead.

"Dude, have you heard anything I've said in the last three minutes?"

"I've heard enough. Do you want me to keep driving or take you back home?" Jasper asked calmly.

Levi shook his head in disbelief. "This is so stupid."

"You're right. Just give me a simple answer. Should I continue on? Yes or no."

Levi crossed his arms over his chest. "Yes."

"If you'd like to fight the whole way there, I'm game," Jasper said. "Or we could strategize what you'll say when you get there."

"Assuming I can even find her."

"Let's stay positive, my man. Are we good? Can we ride in this truck without punching each other?"

Levi nodded.

"Excellent." Jasper turned his blinker on, checked over his shoulder and then merged onto the highway.

They rode in silence until Levi wrestled his pride into submission and spoke first. "I'm sorry I lashed out. Thank you for driving. I shouldn't have snapped at you."

"It's okay. I can take it." Jasper gave him the side eye. "Are you okay, man? You haven't been yourself lately."

Levi blew out a breath and raked his hand through his hair. "I'm sorry that I've been such a lousy brother lately. You and Miranda got engaged, and I haven't exactly been...thrilled."

"Apology accepted." Jasper flashed him a knowing grin. "To be fair, I've been known to not look before I leap. In lots of situations. This time, though, you don't need to worry. I'm in for the long haul. Miranda's the one."

"Glad to hear it," Levi said.

"So, now that we've cleared the air, when we catch up to Savannah, what are you going to say?"

"That I love her? That I need her to stay?"

Jasper rubbed his hand along his stubbly jawline. "What else?"

Levi tipped his head back against the seat. An icy ball of regret lodged in his gut.

"She already felt uneasy about coming back to Opportunity. Her confidence had really tanked."

"Well, now you know why," Jasper said. "I'd

feel lousy, too, if I'd been blamed for something that serious that wasn't my fault."

"Candace didn't help by piling on." Levi glanced at his twin again. "What's her deal, anyway? Why does she stick her nose in everyone's business?"

"Oh, you know Candace." Jasper shrugged. "She's only happiest when she's causing trouble."

"But why is she so good at it?" Levi curled his hands into fists in his lap, getting wound up all over again.

"She preys on people's weaknesses."

"I'm sorry. What?"

Jasper hesitated, drumming his thumb on the steering wheel. "Candace has a knack for figuring out what makes people tick. She uses good old-fashioned sibling rivalry to pit us against each other. Just like she recognizes Savvy's lack of confidence and pokes at her until she gets a reaction."

"You're my twin brother, Jasper. We look out for each other. I'd never throw you under the bus like she did to Savvy."

"You're not wrong," Jasper said. "But Candace can be very convincing. Somehow, she schemes until she's able to point out other people's shortcomings while concealing her own."

Levi huffed out an exasperated breath. "That's so twisted."

Jasper chuckled. "Easy, there. Don't get too indignant now. We've covered this already. That's why we're in this truck, barreling down the highway at a responsible rate of speed."

"Thank you for being the more reasonable, levelheaded twin." Levi reached over and clapped Jasper on the shoulder.

Jasper's mouth twitched. "You know it. Only the most responsible grand gestures for my twin and the love of his life."

Levi's pulse sped up. "Do you think she's the love of my life?"

"I've never seen you go after anybody like this. Even when Tori dumped you, it didn't seem like you tried to do anything to win her back."

"That's not true," Levi insisted. "I couldn't very well argue with someone who wanted to move away from here for her dental-school education."

"Yeah, it's probably better that you two are apart." Jasper accelerated and merged into the left lane to pass an RV ambling down the highway.

Levi tunneled his hand through his hair. "I hate that it took me a while to realize it."

"Getting back on topic," Jasper said, "what are you going to say when we find Savannah?"

Levi stared out the window. He had no idea, even though he'd been thinking of little else. He wanted to tell her that he was sorry for believing Candace and not trusting her. He wanted to let her know that he still loved her and needed her back in his life, despite everything that had happened. Finally, he decided that the best approach would be complete authenticity. He'd tell her his feelings and apologize for any hurtful things he'd said or done. He just hoped it would be enough.

Chapter Eleven

The hotel's automatic doors slid open. Exhaust from the tour bus idling outside as it unloaded passengers drifted in with the cool air. Tourists wandered between the front desk and the elevators, debating their dinner options and peppering the staff with questions about wake-up calls and sightseeing tours. Savannah squinted against the sunlight reflecting off a car in the parking lot as she attempted to steer her luggage cart through the throng of people. Then, standing in her path, was a very familiar face.

Levi. She gasped softly. "What are you doing here?"

His soft blue cotton T-shirt stretched taut across his broad chest, and he wore the same jeans he'd had on at the parade. A mix of surprise and confusion filled his eyes. "Nyla works at the front desk here in the evenings. I stopped by to say hello, but then I saw you."

Why hadn't she picked the hotel across the street instead? What were the chances she'd find an available room where Levi and Jasper's younger sister had a job?

Levi swallowed hard. "When I showed up to the train station in Opportunity and you'd already left, Jasper offered to drive me here and help find you."

He'd tracked her down? Savannah fidgeted with the envelope holding her key as she gazed into Levi's eyes. "But you sided with Candace. You believed her and not me."

She hated that her voice trembled and hurt laced her words. The tension in the air was palpable, like an electric charge filling the space between them.

Levi's jaw tightened, and his forehead creased with frustration. "I shouldn't have jumped to conclusions. It was wrong of me to do that without listening to your side of the story. That's why I'm here—to apologize for my mistake. I am truly sorry, Savannah."

"That still doesn't explain why you would believe anything that Candace has to say. She has a long history of stirring up trouble."

"There was an element of truth to what she said, right? You've been less than honest about a major event that happened to you in the past. An event that could have had a negative impact on me hiring you as a babysitter."

"I lost my job because of a horrible accident. A teenager made a reckless decision that had brutal consequences. I had nothing to do with her death."

"Why didn't you just tell people from the beginning that something terrible had happened?"

"Because I was afraid. I was afraid that no one would believe me. I was afraid I wouldn't get the job because people would automatically assume the worst. And that's exactly what happened, isn't it?"

"It's understandable why people would be cautious after something like this happened, though. You can't blame them for being wary."

"I'm a teacher, Levi. How could you think that I would put a child in danger? Have I done anything to make you doubt me?"

"No, but—"

"Have I given you valuable advice about caring for Wren?"

"Yes, of course."

"Were you ever worried about leaving her with me?"

"No, never."

"But still, you believed Candace without talking to me first."

"I wish you wouldn't put it like that. I was scared and had to consider Wren's safety."

Oh, how she wanted to believe him, but it was hard to forget the doubt that had been cast on her character. "I understand your concern for Wren, but I need to know that you trust me, that you believe in me. Because without that trust, we can't have a relationship."

Levi stepped closer, and the air between them shifted with a sense of longing. "Savannah," he said softly.

She angled the cart away from him and held up her hand. "No, stay where you are." She didn't want to get too close because she wasn't sure if she could trust herself not to let her guard down.

The hurt that flickered in his expression tugged at her heartstrings. "I should have trusted you more. I really care about you, and I want us to try again. For real this time. Will you please forgive me?"

Savannah bit her lip as emotion flooded through her body like waves crashing against the shoreline. She wanted desperately to reach out and take his hands in hers and tell him everything was okay, but fear still lingered like an invisible wall between them. Taking a deep breath, she looked back into his eyes and nodded slowly.

"Yes, I forgive you, but we're not meant to be. Take good care, Levi."

Mercifully, the elevator arrived. An older gentleman stepped off and held the doors open for her. Another couple eased into the back corner, allowing plenty of space. She wheeled her cart inside, intentionally avoiding eye contact with Levi. As the doors closed and she cruised up to her room on the sixth floor, hot tears pressed against the backs of her eyes. She felt betrayed, angry and confused, but now she could add one more sad emotion to the pile—regret. She'd gone and done the one thing she'd hoped to avoid—shattered Levi's fragile heart.

Levi awoke to the sound of his phone ringing and someone knocking on his front door. He wiped fatigue from his gritty eyes and fumbled on his nightstand for the phone.

"No way," he groaned. "It's ten o'clock already?"

Drat. He'd overslept. Dad's name and number lit up the screen.

Pushing up on one elbow, Levi swiped his finger across the glass and took the call. "Hello?"

"Levi? What's going on, man?" Dad's voice carried a trace of concern. "Everything okay?"

"Yeah, I…"

An instant replay from the day before slammed into him with a sickening thud. His emotional conversation with Savvy in the lobby of the hotel. How she'd slipped away after telling him she wasn't interested. Nyla's empathetic expression and gentle hug as she bid him goodbye outside.

Then a very quiet ride back to Opportunity with Jasper.

"Levi? You there?"

"Hang on, Dad. I'll be in as soon as I can, but I gotta take care of Wren first."

"Not a problem," Dad said. "Take your time."

Well, if there was an upside to getting his heart

smashed to pieces, maybe it was gaining some grace and understanding from his father.

He ended the call, threw the covers aside and dragged himself out of bed. Trudging out to the living room, he squinted and looked around. "Wren?"

Hearing no response, terror crept over him. "Wren, let's go! We're late. Have you eaten, or do I need to make breakfast?"

Most days, she left a trail behind her when she tried to get her own cereal without help. His eyes searched across the kitchen. Other than a chair pushed back from the table and angled sideways, nothing suggested anyone had been there recently.

Panic set in. There was a knock on the door. Loud and insistent. He peeked out at the driveway.

Miranda's electric-blue sedan was parked behind his car.

He glanced down at his gym shorts and faded T-shirt. Presentable enough to open the door for Jasper's fiancée. He crossed over to the entryway and reached out to undo the dead bolt. It was already unlocked. His mouth ran dry.

Wren. Had she snuck out unnoticed?

His heart leaped into his throat as he turned the knob and yanked open the door.

Miranda stood on his porch. She'd pulled her hair into a bouncy ponytail, done her makeup, and was wearing cutoff denim jean shorts and a cropped white T-shirt.

"Good morning." Her smile quickly faded as she took in his appearance. "I was supposed to pick Wren up, but I haven't heard from you. Is everything okay?"

Levi scrubbed his hand over his face. That's right. He'd had to ask Miranda to look after Wren that morning because Savvy was gone and he'd run out of options. "Sorry. I overslept and my brain's pretty foggy right now. Wren must still be asleep."

"Oh. Well, do you want me to come back later, then?"

"Actually, if you don't mind, could you just come inside for a second until I'm sure that everything's okay? I don't know if Jasper mentioned anything to you, but we had a rough time yesterday and I'm exhausted."

Miranda's eyes filled with empathy. "Jasper told me. I'm sorry things didn't go like you'd hoped."

"Yeah, me too." He stepped back and motioned for her to come inside. "I'm not sure where Wren is. Let me see if she's still asleep."

"All right." Miranda stood awkwardly inside the door, clutching her purse.

He padded down the hall and tapped softly on Wren's door. It opened with a squeak. "Wren?"

Her bed was empty. His stomach plummeted. *Maybe she's hiding.* "Hey, Wren. Not a great time to play, sweetie. Miranda's here. She came by to pick you up. Are you going fishing today?" He inched closer and pulled back the covers. Her pink-and-white blanket was gone.

"Please, Lord, this can't be," he whispered as he dropped to his knees and looked under the bed. The other night, when he'd tucked her in, his toe had nudged a bag of chips. He'd pretended not to notice but went back later after she'd fallen asleep and found six or seven different snacks stashed under there. Just like Savvy had said. Now that food was gone.

Heart pounding, he scrambled to his feet and circled the room. Maybe she was hiding somewhere else because she was miffed that he'd dropped her off with his mother yesterday so he could make the grueling round trip to Anchorage. Except Mom had said she'd had a ball.

He flung open the closet doors. "Wren, I need you to come out. This isn't funny anymore."

Still no answer. He pushed aside the curtains and peeked into the yard. She wasn't playing out there either. Stumbling into the hall, he pressed his hand to his mouth, trying to contain his rising fear.

Miranda stood next to the sofa, her phone in hand. "Is Wren missing?"

He nodded, then swallowed hard, trying to think. "Where would she go? She's four."

"I'll call Jasper," Miranda said, dropping her keys and her purse on the end of the couch.

"Please do. Tell him to get as many people as

he can together to start searching." Levi turned in another desperate circle. "I'll call the police."

Where had he left his phone? Dad's wake-up call. His nightstand. He hurried into his room, grabbed his phone and called 911.

"911, what's your emergency?"

Levi's stomach twisted into a knot as he gave the emergency operator his address. "My foster daughter is missing," he said, his voice shaking. "I think she might have run away. She's only four years old."

The dispatcher stayed calm and professional. She asked him a few questions about Wren—her eye color, height, hair color—and then told him a patrol car was on its way. After he hung up, he felt numb as he went back into the living room.

Miranda had just ended her call with Jasper.

"Jasper's getting a group together to help search for Wren." She tucked her phone back in her purse. "He thinks she probably just got scared and ran off somewhere nearby. We'll find her soon enough."

Levi nodded but remained silent as Miranda followed him outside and they began walking down the street in search of Wren. He prayed they'd find her safe and sound before anything bad happened to her—because if anything did... He didn't even want to think about it.

She'd only been here three days, and already she'd landed her first interview. Maybe relocating to Anchorage had been meant to be after all. Savannah's heels clicked on the tile as she made her way across the hotel lobby, the smell of fresh coffee and scrambled eggs wafting from the buffet making her stomach rumble. She paused by the bakery case to admire the plump muffins with streusel topping.

Hesitating, she plated eggs and fresh fruit first, then added a muffin and chose a small round table by the window.

Nervous energy hummed through her veins. A large Anchorage high school with an art teacher position and an option to serve as adviser for an extracurricular club sounded ideal. She'd have to figure out housing and probably look for a roommate because she couldn't afford to live here by herself. But she didn't want to blow too much more of her savings living in an expensive hotel either. Add apartment hunting to her growing list of things to do.

If she got the job.

She poured coffee with a dash of cream and sugar into her cup and returned to her table. Nyla was waiting for her.

"Nyla." Savannah hesitated, then slowly sank into her chair. "Good morning."

Dark circles and a wrinkled uniform hinted at Nyla's exhaustion. "Hey."

"Are you doing okay? I hear working the night shift is rough."

"It's not too bad," Nyla said, yawning. "Listen, I need to talk to you."

Savannah eyed her, a forkful of scrambled eggs halfway to her mouth. "If Levi asked you to talk to me, I don't think that's a good idea. I've said—"

"No."

Savannah leaned back, startled by Nyla's terse interruption. "What do you mean, 'no'?"

"This isn't about Levi. Well, it sort of is." Nyla shook her head. "Wow, I'm so tired, I can't even make sense. Savvy, I hate to tell you this first thing in the morning, but Wren is missing."

Savannah's mouth ran dry. Her fork slipped from her hand and clattered to the floor. "What?"

"Yeah, I know. Terrifying, right? Levi woke up yesterday morning and Wren was gone."

Savannah frowned. "Yesterday morning? Why am I just now finding out about it?"

Nyla pinned her with a long look. "Because you kind of told my brother you didn't want anything to do with him."

"I know, but a missing child is a big deal."

"That's why I'm here. We were hoping you would have some ideas about where she might be."

"Me?" Savannah pressed her hand to her chest. "Um, I have no idea. But she couldn't have gone far. She's four and not all that independent."

"That's what has everyone so concerned," Nyla said. "I've made arrangements for someone to cover my shift, and I borrowed a car from my roommate. We could be back in Opportunity by lunchtime, if you're willing to join the search."

Savannah picked at the cardboard sleeve ringing her disposable coffee cup. "I don't know, Nyla. I mean, I just got here, and I have an interview today for a teaching position—plus, I need to find a place to live."

Nyla's mouth drifted open.

"That sounds harsh, but it's true. And I'm afraid if I go back home, that'll just be extra upsetting for everyone."

"You don't have to stay," Nyla said softly. "We're just asking you to help look for Wren. I haven't spent much time with her, but my parents have told me how much you meant to her and to Levi. I don't think he would have made it through these last few weeks without you."

Savvy looked away. "That's sweet of you to say. I was glad to help, and I'm thankful that I got to be a part of Wren's life, even for a little while."

Unexpected emotions clogged her throat.

"So you'll help? Come on." Nyla stood and pushed in her chair. "I'll help you put your stuff in my roommate's car."

Savannah remained seated. In the background, a phone at the desk rang. The call button on the elevator dinged, and an elderly couple shuffled in.

Worry flickered in Nyla's eyes. "I'm sure if you tell the people who want to interview you that you've had a family emergency, they will understand. I promise I'll drive you back."

Savvy stared out the window at the morning traffic cruising through downtown. A woman and a young girl walked hand in hand on the sidewalk, pausing to look at a large planter overflowing with gorgeous flowers.

The horror of what had happened in Colorado came rushing back, making her stomach churn. She hadn't forgotten how terrible it was—the waiting and the not knowing. Especially if the outcome wasn't what you'd hoped. She banished that morbid thought. They'd find Wren. This story had to have a happy ending.

Besides, if she was honest, she already regretted telling Levi that she didn't want him. Even if they couldn't repair what had broken between them, she could show up. Make the effort to find that precious little girl.

"All right." She stood and gathered her coffee and uneaten breakfast. "If you'll help me pack my stuff, I'll take this to go, and we can be on the road within the hour."

Relief spread across Nyla's face. Her hazel eyes, so similar to her brother's, and the way they lit up when she smiled made Savannah want to get home even sooner.

"Let's go." Nyla gently squeezed Savannah's arm as they strode toward the elevator. "We're all in this together. Our people need us."

* * *

"We will find her." Adele, Pastor Blanchett's wife, pressed a second disposable cup of coffee into Levi's hands. He offered a thin smile. "Thank you."

Shifting his weight from one foot to the other, he didn't have the heart to tell her she wasn't the first one to bring him mediocre coffee or a kind word that morning. He stood under the tent they'd put up in the park across the street from the library. The same park where Wren had hid in the jungle gym after her story-time disaster. The same park where he'd sat on the swings and Savvy had helped him formulate a plan for how to help Wren.

"We're praying for you, sweetie." Connie, Mrs. Blanchett's sister, squeezed his arm, then tucked a card—probably with a verse printed on it—inside his coat pocket. A cool breeze rustled through the trees at the edge of the property. He shivered and forced himself to sip the coffee.

Grimacing, he tried to focus on the chatter filtering through the walkie-talkies nearby. It was a little after 10:00 a.m., and the search for Wren continued. Volunteers and trained staff from emergency services had canvassed Opportunity.

The women's peaceful and serene presence reminded him that people were not only searching but also praying.

"Thank you." He cleared his throat, battling back the emotion that threatened to take him down. He had to stay strong, though. They were going on twenty-six hours since he'd discovered Wren was missing. Doubt had weaseled its way in, picking at him, filling his head with horrifying thoughts. Where could one little four-year-old hide for a whole day?

The canine team and their handlers approached with their panting dogs. Levi averted his gaze. His mother picked her way across the dew-soaked grass, carrying a breakfast sandwich wrapped in paper from Riverside Café.

"You need to eat, honey. Keep your strength up."

He leaned down and kissed her cheek. "Thanks, Mom." He took the sandwich, but his stomach roiled. Almost like he'd forgotten how to eat— how to do much of anything, really, since Wren had vanished. All he could think about was how scared Wren would be if a German shepherd came at her with its pink tongue lolling. But they said the dogs were the best resource they had. He couldn't argue with that.

A van with the words *Swift Water Rescue Team* on the side pulled up to the curb.

He had to turn away and choke back a sob. "Oh, sweetheart." His mother looped her arm around his waist. "I know this is hard."

"She can't be in the river, Mom," his voice rasped as he squeezed the words out. "She just can't be."

"We're praying that she's safe and that she is just holed up somewhere," Mom said, her eyes glassy with tears.

"But why? Why would she hide? Is this because of me? Is it something I've said?"

"Nonsense. You're a bright spot in that little girl's world. We don't know why little children who've seen trauma do what they do," she said. "Kids run off all the time."

He scoffed. "Not all the time. We never ran away."

"Oh, sure you did. You and your brothers built a fort, camped out there and refused to come home. Then Nyla went to your grandparents' house because I wouldn't let her buy a red lipstick in second grade."

"Wait." He set the coffee and breakfast sandwich down on the table nearby. "Why didn't we think of that? Has anyone looked at Grandma and Grandpa's house yet?"

Mom's eyes searched his. "What are you saying?"

He wiped at his nose with the back of his hand, then fumbled in his pockets for his phone.

"When we find her—because we will find her—I hope she'll be able to tell you why. But you cannot lose hope," Mom reminded him.

"It's so hard keeping track of all the details." He turned in a circle, looking for the team lead han-

dling the search for the day. "Are we sure someone looked in the barn?"

Mom's brow furrowed. "I—I don't know. Let's
get you some water."

She turned and retrieved a bottle from the dozens people had donated. Food had piled up on a
card table nearby. Women stood in a circle near
the swings, holding hands, heads bowed.

He hadn't slept for more than a couple of hours
since Wren had disappeared. Fatigue clung to him,
and his eyes burned. But how could he rest when
she was still missing? Between the volunteers who
were praying, the men and women who'd been
searching around the clock, and now the volunteers from the fire department and the police station who had joined forces to search, there was
no way they would leave even one single fort or
shed or pile of rocks unturned.

Except he couldn't shake the niggling thought
that maybe no one had been by the barn where
Wren had hung out when they'd worked on the
parade float. He bowed his head and closed his
weary eyes. "Lord, please. I love this little girl so
much. Calm her fears. If she's running, turn her
around. Bring somebody alongside her who can
guide her safely home. Amen."

The crackle came through the radio. He heard
the words, but didn't believe them. Not at first.

"Found her."

Then his phone rang, buried under a fleece

blanket someone had dropped off earlier. His mom's phone hummed with an incoming text. The news spread in rings and tones and gasps of surprise, like church bells chiming on a Sunday morning. Relieved smiles turned his way, and suddenly he was being swarmed.

"Levi, they found her! They found Wren. Did you hear?"

People slapped him on the back, patted his cheeks, then grabbed his elbow and hauled him toward a strange vehicle as it stopped in the middle of the street.

"They found her. Levi, you'll never believe where," someone said.

Nyla stepped out. Then the back door opened slowly, and Wren scrambled out. His breath left his lungs in a desperate gust of shock. She ran toward him, tears streaming down her filthy face and her little arms outstretched.

"Wren!" He scooped her up and whirled her around. "You're back. I'm so glad. Oh, thank God."

"I'm sorry, Lee-by. I'm really sorry." She sobbed into his shoulder.

"It's okay, sweetie. I'm just so glad you've been found." He leaned away and smoothed her hair from her eyes. "Can you tell me why you ran away?"

Shame flitted across her face, and she dipped her chin.

"You can tell me. I won't be angry," he said softly.

"I heard you say to your mom that Sabby was gone, and I got scared and mad 'cuz I need her. After you went to sleep, I sneaked away."

Oh. Her words pierced him. *You're not the only one who needs Savvy, kiddo.* "I'm sorry that you had to hear about Savannah leaving that way. Next time you hear something that scares you, please come to me, okay?"

She nodded. "'Kay."

"Who found you?"

"Sabby did, silly." Wren swiped her hand across her face and twisted in his arms and pointed.

Savannah stood crying beside Nyla, their arms wrapped around each other. His vision blurred, and he made his way through the crowd that parted till he was standing in front of Savvy.

Wren clung to him.

"Savvy, you came," he said, sniffling.

She nodded and wiped at her cheeks with her fingertips. "On a whim, I asked Nyla to pull into your grandparents' place. They weren't home. But I found Wren hanging out in the truck in the barn."

"It's a good hiding spot," Wren said, "but I was getting really hungry."

He'd been fairly sure his grandparents' place had been searched at the outset—all the spots Wren was familiar with had been looked into. He wondered if the sound of strangers had scared her, though, and she'd burrowed under a blanket in the truck, quiet and still.

His tears turned into laughter. He had a million questions to ask the little girl, but for now, he couldn't take his eyes off Savannah. "Thank you," he said. "Truly, you have no idea how grateful I am."

Her chin wobbled. "When Nyla told me Wren had gone missing, I was so conflicted. I didn't even know if you'd want me here."

"It took some persuading," Nyla said, "but I got her in the car."

Pain flashed in Savannah's eyes. "Levi, I'm so sorry."

Nyla stepped away, linking her arm through their mother's. "Let's give them a little space, okay?"

"Wait." He shifted Wren to his other hip. "Savvy, I need to tell you something."

"I need to tell you a lot of somethings," Wren said, stretching her hands wide. "Starting with I wuv you both."

He was done for. Another wave of tears crested. He held out his arm, and Savannah closed the distance between them.

"Levi, I'm so sorry for what I said to you in the hotel. You poured your heart out, and I was so cruel." She stared up at him. "Will you forgive me?"

"Absolutely." His eyes drifted toward her lips.

"I love you, Savannah Morgan. I can't imagine my life without you in it."

"I love you too," Savvy whispered.

Wren clasped her hands under her chin. "You should kiss."

"She's right," Savvy said.

"What a clever kid," he said, leaning down and brushing a tender kiss across Savannah's lips.

"Yay!" Wren cheered.

Laughter rippled through the crowd as the people of Opportunity celebrated a lost little girl who'd maybe, just maybe, found her forever family.

Epilogue

Two years later

Savannah waved until the school bus had pulled out of the church parking lot and turned onto the highway, disappearing around the bend. As she watched it go, the circle of moms that had gathered to see the kids off to camp erupted into a flurry of high fives and excited chatter about their long-awaited girls' weekend. Blinking back tears, she turned away and walked back to her car, gripping the key chain holding the photo of her with Levi and Wren. Their sweet girl. So brave going to church camp near Anchorage for a whole week. Savannah had never been that brave when she was six years old. She kept her chin low as she passed the trio of moms, a few stray tears sliding down her cheeks.

Slipping in behind the wheel, Savannah sighed as she closed the door. She had been so emotional lately, more so than usual. But then, why wouldn't she be? Just this morning, she had taken a test that she knew would change her life.

Levi's too. She couldn't wait to tell him. He was going to be over the moon.

The drive home was a blur, and eerily quiet without Wren in the back seat, chatting away. Savannah slowed at the entrance to her parents' neighborhood. She couldn't wait to tell them, her sisters and Wyatt that her pregnancy test had come back positive. They were going to have a baby. She was still in shock, her mind racing with all the implications of this new development. But amid her anxiety, there was an unmistakable joy too. The joy of new life and new possibilities. She had to reconnect with Levi first. Then they'd decide how and when to announce their incredible news.

As she pulled into the driveway, Savannah spotted Levi on the front porch of his A-frame, waiting for her. She had called him before leaving to drop Wren off at the church and to let him know that she needed him to meet her at the house. Now that he owned the store and had hired an incredible manager, he didn't feel quite so compelled to spend every minute there. His father had retired a year ago, and Jasper had decided retail wasn't his life's calling. Instead, he'd gone back to college to earn his teaching degree.

Savannah parked and got out of the car, walking slowly toward Levi, who had a huge smile on his face. As she got closer to him, he opened his arms wide, and she climbed the steps and walked into his familiar embrace. It felt like coming home after a long journey. Like everything was exactly as it should be in that moment in time. As he held her, Savannah could feel both happiness and gratitude washing over them both. They hadn't planned to start a family quite this soon. What a sweet surprise for a pair of newlyweds.

They stood there for what felt like forever, until finally Levi pulled away slightly and looked into Savannah's eyes with love and adoration. "Mrs. Carter, are we going to have a baby?"

"We sure are, Mr. Carter." She pressed up on her tiptoes and kissed him tenderly. "How did you know?"

"Someone saw you buying a pregnancy test at the store and sent me a text." He winked and offered her his arm. "Let's go inside and enjoy a peaceful kid-free home while we can."

For once she didn't mind that good news had traveled quickly. In a gesture reminiscent of their very memorable fake date at the Fairview two summers ago, she tucked her fingers into the crook of his elbow and followed him through the front door.

Some wise folks in their lives had counseled them not to rush into anything. And sometimes, she wondered if they'd worked a little too hard at disregarding that advice. Because the last two years had not been easy. She'd moved back to Opportunity less than a week after she'd left. Mr. Schubert hired her for the art teacher position, after apologizing profusely for enabling Candace's schemes. He'd probably never admit it, but he'd given her the highly coveted role of advising the students who designed the yearbook, a gesture she was certain was one made out of guilt. Not that his decision bothered her one bit. She loved teaching and advising, and the yearbook had been stunning. Then Levi had proposed the following spring, and they'd eloped in Hawaii last Christmas during her school break. She'd put her feet on Honolulu's sugary sand after all.

Sadly, Wren's mom had not been able to conquer her addiction. After her arrest and lengthy prison sentence, her parental rights were terminated. Wren became eligible for adoption after her father had passed away almost a year ago. Levi and Savannah had walked a hard road with the spunky little girl, helping her work through her grief. They'd spent countless hours in therapy, attended hearings and signed what seemed like more than a hundred pieces of paper, until Wren's formal adoption had been finalized six months ago.

"Wren is going to flip out," Levi said, pushing aside a small mountain of stuffed animals she'd discarded on the couch before she'd left that morning. He sat down on the cushions and patted the space beside him. Savannah nestled in beside her sweet husband and rested her head on his shoulder. "Are you hoping for a boy or a girl?"

He hesitated, then twined his fingers through hers. "I'm hoping for a healthy baby. You?"

"Healthy, yes." She squeezed his strong, calloused hand. "I'd love for Wren to have a sister because Hayley and Juliet have brought so much joy to my life. But I see how much fun you and Jasper have together, and I appreciate how Wyatt has looked out for me over the years, and I don't know… Brothers are amazing too."

She trailed off as Levi's eyes darkened. "Brothers, huh? As in, plural?"

Her pulse sped up as he inched closer. "There's only one baby in my tummy at the moment."

"Oh, darlin', we're just getting started." He claimed her mouth with his, and she lost all logical thought as he swept her away with a passionate kiss.

She'd never imagined being a mom with a houseful of kids. But loving Levi and Wren, and getting married, had taught her that life was full of surprises. In the distance, the train whistle bellowed, and Savannah remembered sweet Martha, the lovely stranger who'd graciously come alongside her on a dark day, encouraged her not to lose hope and reminded her that God still had a remarkable plan for her life.

Good call, Martha. Good call.

* * * * *

*Look for Heidi McCahan's next book,
a full-length novel from Love Inspired Trade,
coming in March 2025!*

Dear Reader,

I'm so excited to introduce you to this new mini-series set in the fictional community of Opportunity, Alaska. To be honest, I didn't initially set out to write a book about a character who struggles with a "mean girl." But as the story unfolded, I really explored how we're supposed to live among folks whose words and actions get under our skin.

Isn't it interesting how fictional stories and imaginary settings often reflect issues we're dealing with in our real lives? Much like Savannah and Levi, I needed a reminder of how God encourages us to love difficult people and extend grace. Writing this story also reminded me of God's promise that we don't need to be ashamed of our mistakes. He is waiting for us with open arms, even when we're determined to solve problems on our own. As always, my hope is that reading this novel will inspire you to reflect on the truths found in God's Word and strengthen your relationship with Him.

I hope you enjoyed your visit to Opportunity, and I look forward to sharing another story soon. Thank you for supporting Christian fiction and telling your friends how much you enjoy our books. I'd love to connect with you. You can find me online: www.Facebook.com/heidimccahan/, heidimccahan.com/

or www.Instagram.com/heidimccahan.author. For news about book releases and sales, sign up for my author newsletter: www.subscribepage.com/heidimccahan-newoptin.

Until next time,
Heidi